"Want to go into the bedroom, cowboy?" Jo asked breathlessly

"Not yet, sweet thing." Russ reached for the front catch of her bra. "There's a lot we can get done right here." He flicked her bra open with a practiced hand and gently moved the material aside as his gaze lowered. "Now, if that ain't a mighty fine sight." He brushed his thumb lazily back and forth across her nipple.

She closed her eyes, wondering how long her legs would support her.

"Ah, sweetheart, you're shaking already, aren't you?"

Jo opened her eyes and looked up. Never in her life had she felt so vulnerable. Never had a man brought her to the brink with just the look in his eyes and the casual stroke of his thumb.

His warm smile and soft voice flowed over her. "Don't be scared. It's good to want someone like this. Some folks never let themselves."

She swallowed. "Do…you?"

"I sure do," he said. Then, with his lips near her ear, he whispered, *"In fact, I'm fixin' to wear you out…."*

Dear Reader,

When you were five years old, you were probably pretty excited at the thought of a jolly old elf bringing you loads of presents on Christmas Eve. But let's face it, you're not five anymore and your taste in men has changed. So, this year, instead of a chubby guy in a red suit, I thought I'd offer you something you might like better—a drop-dead gorgeous cowboy to be your resident Santa for this special night of the year.

Russ Gibson, my Santa in a Stetson, will arrive on your doorstep with his own sleigh and a smile that will charm your socks off. Although December 24 is one of the shortest nights of the year, this sexy cowboy knows how to make every second count. I've always been told that the best presents are those you'd like to receive yourself. So in that spirit, here's Russ, with my warmest wishes for a sensual Christmas Eve and a delectable holiday season.

Happy Holidays,

Vicki Lewis Thompson

P.S. My love affair with cowboys continues into the New Year with *Manhunting in Montana,* an April 1998 release. Join me…again.

Vicki Lewis Thompson
SANTA IN A STETSON

Harlequin Books

TORONTO • NEW YORK • LONDON
AMSTERDAM • PARIS • SYDNEY • HAMBURG
STOCKHOLM • ATHENS • TOKYO • MILAN
MADRID • WARSAW • BUDAPEST • AUCKLAND

For my editor, Brenda Chin, who has
renewed my faith in Santa Claus.
Merry Christmas, Brenda.

ISBN 0-373-25761-9

SANTA IN A STETSON

Copyright © 1997 by Vicki Lewis Thompson.

Printed in U.S.A.

1

BEING DUMPED right after Thanksgiving had been a blessing.

Most times Jo Cassidy believed that. But tonight, exactly one year to the day since Tommy had grabbed his hat off the peg by the door and walked out, Jo was bluer than a new pair of jeans. She did her best to hide it. The cowboys who hung out at Prescott's Roundup Saloon didn't much care for gloomy waitresses, and she needed all the tips she could earn.

"Hey, Jo, we could use another round," called a grizzled old cowhand who had a hot game of pool going with one of his friends.

"Coming up, Andy." Jo deposited napkins and two long-necks in front of a couple of men sitting at a table by the jukebox. Then she hurried to the bar to fill Andy's order.

Lots of folks had gone to Phoenix to start their Christmas shopping, which cut down on business tonight. The boss had already told her she could go home early, but the prospect of her empty apartment didn't thrill her much. If only something good would happen, something *really* good, it might cancel out the memory of Tommy's battered pickup pulling away for good and the buckets of tears she'd cried until dawn.

"Have a good Thanksgivin', Jo?" Andy asked as she handed him a beer.

"Fine, thanks," Jo lied. Andy wouldn't approve of her microwaved turkey dinner. "How about you?" she asked, walking around the pool table to deliver a second one to Andy's friend, Snuffy.

"It was okay." Andy took a swig of his beer. "Knowin' you, you probably spent the day with your nose in your schoolbooks."

Bingo. Tommy's rodeo prize money had been earmarked for her schooling, but it turned out Tommy liked to gamble, so now she was earning her own way. She'd chosen Yavapai College because it put more than a thousand miles and the Grand Canyon between her and her ex-husband, who was still drinking and gambling his life away in Montana. "Finals are coming up, Andy," she said. "I'm planning on making the dean's list."

Andy grinned. "The dean's list? Did you hear that, Snuffy?"

Snuffy spat into the tin can by his elbow. "Guess we'll hafta call you professor pretty soon."

"Nope. Doctor. I'm going to be a horse vet, but that's a lot of years away," she said.

"A vet, huh?" Andy said. "That don't make you squeamish, all that blood and stuff?"

"Not when I think of an animal needing help. I've wanted to do this ever since I was a kid and helped my dad deliver a foal. It was so young and helpless." She shrugged. "I've always been a softie when it came to animals. What better career could I choose?"

"We could always use a good horse vet around here," Andy said. "'Course, then you'll be too high-toned to talk to the likes of us."

"That'll never happen." She flashed Andy a grin. Little did he know how much she treasured the conversations she had with her customers. She'd left her folks back in Montana, too. Between classes and working at the Roundup, she hadn't had much time for socializing, which meant she got awfully lonesome sometimes. Tonight was one of those times.

When she noticed rancher Steve Gibson walk through the door of the Roundup, her spirits lifted considerably. Steve was one of her favorites, especially after she found out that he and his wife, Claire, spent Christmas Eve delivering surprise gifts to folks who were short on cash or joy. Jo's neighbor, Lucile, qualified on both counts, and Jo had been waiting for Steve to show up so she could tell him about Lucile.

Ned Kershaw, a beefy cowhand who was getting married next month, came in behind Steve, but it was the stranger following Ned who nearly made Jo lose her grip on her serving tray. She'd seen her share of good-looking cowboys. Tommy had been no slouch in that department. But the tall, dark-eyed hombre in the black Stetson had them all beat.

He unbuttoned his sheepskin coat as he accompanied Ned and Steve to the corner table Steve always occupied. Then he shrugged out of it, revealing a spotless white shirt and a black suede vest embroidered with a feather design that emphasized his broad shoulders. Jo took in every detail, from the tilt of his hat to the shine on his belt buckle. Then he laughed, the sound rich and low, and goose bumps prickled her skin.

"Andy, who's that who just came in with Steve and Ned?" she asked.

Andy squinted across the room. "Looks like Russ, Steve's brother."

"Ain't he the one that galloped his horse up the courthouse steps last summer, just for the heck of it?" Snuffy asked.

"He's the one," Andy said.

"So that's Russ Gibson." Jo had heard stories about him, but nobody had mentioned he was a hunk. It was a serious omission.

Folks said he was a loner, a rolling stone who helped Steve with his horseshoeing business in the summer and worked for a dude ranch in Tucson during the winter. Rumor had it that Russ was wild, proven by the fact that he had no driver's license, leaving many to speculate as to what reckless act he'd committed. He didn't talk much about himself, and to the residents of Prescott, that meant he was hiding some dark secret.

"Don't go losin' your heart to Russ Gibson, girl," Andy said.

Jo was startled out of her daze. So what if Russ was gorgeous? She had no time for romance, and no good-looking cowboy would cheat her out of her dream this time. She glanced at Andy. "My heart belongs to you, handsome."

Andy grinned. "I always knowed that." Then his grin faded. "Steve's steady as they come, but I guess it don't run in the family. From what I hear, his brother is the love-'em-leave-'em type."

"Don't worry, Andy." Jo patted his arm. "No fancy cowboy is going to keep me from getting my degree. I want it too bad. But I have to earn a living, so I'm going over there to find out what those gentlemen are having."

"Jist consider yourself warned."

"Thanks, I will." Jo adjusted her uniform and took a deep breath as she crossed the room. The Roundup dressed their waitresses in a style that reminded Jo of a Dallas Cowboys' cheerleader, with tight little shorts, white boots, hat and a snug-fitting top that displayed a generous amount of cleavage. It was a sexist outfit, but it sure brought in good tips, so Jo put up with it.

Approaching Russ Gibson, she had the insane urge to cover up. She'd easily sidestepped the passes made by other cowboys in the months she'd worked at the Roundup, but none of them had affected her like this. Maybe her reaction to Russ had to do with her mood tonight. She'd wished something really good would happen to erase her memory of Tommy leaving, but getting involved with a stud who specialized in breaking hearts could make everything worse. She'd have to be careful.

RUSS NOTICED HER the minute he walked into the Roundup, and something told him he ought to convince Steve and Ned to try a different bar tonight. But he knew how much they liked the Roundup and they wouldn't appreciate being dragged down the block for reasons he couldn't even put into words.

The waitresses in the Roundup were always very pretty—and stacked. Russ knew that Eddie Johnson, the owner, made sure of that. Eddie tended to hire blondes, but not this time around, apparently. Her long, shiny hair reminded Russ of the brownish-red coat on a chestnut mare he'd once owned. That mare had been a favorite of his, and he'd been attracted to that hair color on a woman ever since. The waitress reminded him of the beautiful horse in another way, too—the way she carried herself. The mare had moved as if announcing she was part Thoroughbred, and so did the waitress. He'd bet she didn't plan to be serving drinks to cowhands for the rest of her life.

Russ pretended not to notice as she came over to take their order, but damned if she didn't stand right beside him, her flowery scent filling his head and her creamy thigh only inches from his arm.

"What can I get for you gentlemen tonight?" she asked.

The sound of her voice, music that rippled down his spine, brought his head up and he looked into smoky green eyes. Lord, he shouldn't have done that. Behind the intelligence, behind the determination he'd sensed the first time he saw her, was a deep sadness. Only someone who also nursed an open wound would see it, and it drew him like a moth to a flame.

"Jo, I'd like you to meet my little brother, Russ," Steve said. "Russ, this is Jo Cassidy."

Russ pushed back his chair and stood. "Glad to meet you, ma'am," he said, touching the brim of his hat. He liked looking at her from this angle, too. Her mouth was wide and generous, just right for kissing. Not that he'd be doing any of that. She was way too classy for the likes of him.

"Nice meeting you, Russ." Her cheeks turned all pink as she glanced up at him.

Russ swallowed. Darned if she wasn't reacting to him the same way he'd reacted to her. But the confusion in her eyes told him she was fighting it, just as he was.

"Russ decided to give us the honor of his company for Thanksgiving," Steve said.

"That's nice." Jo continued to stare into Russ's eyes.

"Jo's studyin' to be a horse vet," Ned added.

"Well, I have to get my degree first," Jo said, continuing to hold Russ's gaze. "Then I'll apply to veterinary schools."

"You must be a real smart lady," Russ said.

"I just hope I'm smart enough." She finally seemed to find the strength to look away. "Right now I'd better

quit jabbering and do my job. The usual for you two?"
she asked Steve and Ned.

"That'll be fine," Steve said.

"Russ?" She glanced up at him. "What'll you have?"

His mind answered one way, but he managed not to
say the words out loud. "A draft will do fine, thanks."

"I'll be right back."

He stood there like an idiot watching her walk toward
the bar.

"You can plant yer butt in the chair, now," Ned said.
"The lady's left."

With a sheepish grin, Russ sat down and adjusted his
hat.

"Hey, little brother, don't mess with her," Steve said.
"She's a real nice girl and is working hard to get through
college. She doesn't need her heart broke right now."

"What makes you think I'd do a thing like that?"

Steve held up his work-roughened hand and started
ticking off names on his fingers. "Ellen last summer,
Beth last fall, Suzanne down in Tucson, Amy in Phoenix.
You're leavin' a trail of them through the state. Not a one
of them means a thing to you, do they?"

"They were all nice girls, but...I'm just not settlin'
down, is all. I'll leave that to you and Ned."

"That bein' the case, I hope you'll stay away from Jo.
She deserves somebody who'll hang around for a while,
like about fifty or sixty years."

Steve was absolutely right, he knew, but Russ didn't
appreciate the lecture. He'd thought about staying in
Prescott another week or so, but maybe that wasn't such
a good idea. "Don't worry, big brother. I'm taking the
bus back to Tucson on Sunday, so I won't have much
time to mess with her, as you put it."

"Sunday?" Ned asked. "But you just got here."

"Yeah," Steve said. "Claire was hoping you'd stay through Christmas, at least."

"No way. You know damned well I don't do Christmas."

Ned leaned forward. "Okay, I have to ask. This purely puzzles me. Here's Steve and Claire runnin' around every Christmas Eve bringing presents to folks, and here's you, finding some hole to crawl into until the holiday's over. What's your problem with Christmas, Russ?"

A steel gate clanged shut in his heart. "Just not into it," he said woodenly.

Steve cleared his throat. "By the way, Ned, are we gonna have a bachelor party for you or what? Eddie said we could reserve the Roundup if we want, and all we have to do is start plannin' it. The night before the rehearsal dinner would be best."

Russ sent his brother a look of thanks. Steve might not like the way he was running his life, but he wouldn't let anyone, not even a good friend like Ned, pry into his little brother's private hell. Nobody except Steve and Claire knew what had happened in New Mexico three Christmases ago, and they'd promised to keep it to themselves.

Ned glanced from Steve to Russ and back to Steve again. Then he shrugged. "Sounds good to me. Claire's planning a shower for Sharon the night before the rehearsal dinner, so we might as well have the bachelor party at the same time."

"Ol' Ned, a married man," Russ said, clapping him on the back. "Who would've believed it?"

Ned gazed at him. "Happens to most of us, sooner or later. Some sweet thing might lasso you yet, Russ."

"Not likely." Russ sensed more than heard Jo approach. His body went on alert, picking up her fragrance and relaying the message to his brain that she was too close for comfort. His blood pumped a little faster.

"A draft," she said, setting down a napkin and putting a frosty glass in front of him.

"Thank you kindly."

"A lemonade, and a long-neck," she continued, putting the lemonade in front of Steve, who hated the taste of liquor and only came into bars for the company.

As she leaned down to deliver the drinks, Russ caught a glimpse of shadowed cleavage and desire became a sweet throbbing in his groin.

"Do you gentlemen want me to run a tab?" she asked, holding her tray against her hip.

"That'd be fine," Steve said. "If Andy ever finishes that game with Snuffy, we might even shoot some pool tonight. Claire and Sharon drove to Phoenix to do some Christmas shopping and won't be back 'til tomorrow, so we're footloose."

"By all means make yourselves at home," Jo said, not looking at Russ.

He had the feeling she'd decided to avoid eye contact with him, which was a good thing for both of them. But she was standing right beside his chair, and damned if he couldn't feel her heat. He clenched his jaw.

"By the way, Steve," she said. "Do you have room for another person on your Christmas Eve gift list?"

Steve laughed. "Sure. What can we bring you, Jo?"

"Not for me. But Lucile Varnum, the widow who lives on the other side of my duplex, could use some cheering up."

"We can probably fit in one more, depending on what you think she needs."

"Well, it might be hard to find this time of year, but

her old cat just died, and she's so lonesome. I was thinking that if you knew anybody who has a kitten, it
would—"

"If that don't beat all," Ned said, turning to Steve.
"Here you was cussin' about that barn cat having babies
so late you have to keep 'em in the house so they won't
freeze, and here's somebody who needs one."

"You really have kittens?" Jo said.

"'Bout four weeks old," Steve said. "I told Claire
they'd be perfect for Christmas presents, but she said
nobody on our list needed a kitten, so it looked like we
were gonna be stuck with them. What do you think
about givin' her two, so they could keep each other company?"

"Watch out," Russ said, glancing up at her. "In a minute Steve's gonna try to unload all five of them, two for
your neighbor and three for you."

Jo's gaze skittered over him. "Between school and
work I'm not home enough to give them the right kind
of attention. Otherwise I'd take them in a minute. I miss
having animals around. Back in Montana, my folks have
everything—dogs, cats, chickens, baby goats. And of
course, horses."

A Montana girl, he thought, intrigued. He'd never
known anybody from Montana. He'd always wanted to
see the place. "How come you ended up down here?"

The sadness flickered again in her green eyes. "The
college looked good, and I—wanted to see what Arizona
was like."

He'd bet there was a lot more to it than that. A woman
didn't up and leave home for the hell of it. Chances
were, she'd tried to run away from something painful
back in Montana, the way he'd tried to run away from a
whole lot of pain back in New Mexico. She'd have to

find out on her own that running away didn't help much.

"Claire's spoilin' those kittens something awful," Steve said. "But I can guarantee they'll be really tame."

"They sound perfect for Lucile. She treated Pookie like a queen."

"Then consider it a done deal," Steve said.

Jo gave Russ another tentative glance. "Will you be helping Steve and Claire this year?"

He felt a stab of regret at the hopeful expression on her face. She was probably wondering if he fit into the nice-guy category. She might as well find out the truth now. "No, I won't."

"Russ don't do Christmas," Ned said. "And I just found out he don't want to talk about the subject, neither."

"Oh. I see."

If he'd expected to push her away with that information, it wasn't working. Instead, she looked at him with new interest, as if he was a puzzle she'd like to solve. That wasn't good, because the interest in her eyes was doing terrible things to his plan to stay away from her.

"I've got nothin' against Thanksgiving," he said softly.

"Is that right?" A soft smile lit her face.

"Looks like Andy's finally fixin' to give up that pool table," Steve said. "And I'm in the mood to whip your butt, Russ. Ned can take the winner, which is gonna be me."

Russ looked at his brother. He knew good and well what Steve was doing. He figured Russ wouldn't be able to back down from a challenge, which would get him away from Jo. Well, that was for the best, although Steve's interference was beginning to grate on his nerves. He'd never seen his brother so concerned about his love life.

Russ pushed back his chair and picked up his beer. "Better pick out a good stick, big brother. You're gonna need it."

"Thanks again for the kittens, Steve." Jo moved away from the table. "You boys just holler when you're ready for another round."

She was no sooner out of earshot than Steve started in on Russ.

"Doggone it, son, what're you thinkin'?" Steve said in an undertone. "Jo is not the kind of woman you stage a one-night stand with."

"I never said I was planning on that," Russ said, irritated now. "I'm just flirting with her a little, is all. How come you're so worried all of a sudden? I've been flirting with women most all my life and I don't recall you getting all hot and bothered about it."

"I didn't know most of 'em, I guess." Steve glanced back at Ned, who'd stopped to talk to somebody on the way to the pool table. "Ned and I come into the Roundup two, maybe three times a week, and Jo's always here, working like crazy. She misses her family, but they don't have the money to come here to visit and she's saving every penny she can lay her hands on for tuition, so she can't afford to go up there."

"And that's another thing." Russ took a cue stick down from the wall and sighted along it. "There's colleges in Montana. How come she had to travel all the way to Arizona for this education of hers? She wouldn't have to miss her family if she'd stayed in Montana."

Steve racked the balls. "From little things she's said, I figure some cowboy did her wrong back home. But whatever happened, she's got grit, comin' down here all by herself and workin' her way through school."

"Then maybe she's got enough grit to handle a varmint like me." Russ chalked the tip of his cue.

"If I thought you'd take the whole thing seriously, I'd be all for it, but I don't think you would."

"You're right about that. I don't take any woman seriously. Not anymore."

"Dammit, Russ. When are you going to—"

"Want me to break?" Russ interrupted.

Steve stepped away from the pool table with a sigh. "Be my guest."

Russ leaned over the table, lined up his stick and sent the cue ball rocketing across the green felt. It smashed into the orderly lineup of colored balls with a crack that could be heard even above the sound of Garth Brooks on the jukebox. Three balls dropped in the pockets, then Russ proceeded to clean the table, never giving Steve a shot.

When it was over, he glanced at his brother with a brief smile. "Now pool, that's something I take very seriously."

2

JO KEPT ONE EYE on the cowboy dominating the pool table as she circulated through the room taking orders and delivering drinks. Russ might be the wild Gibson brother, but he was definitely more interesting than good old dependable Steve. Jo recognized a kindred spirit in Russ, a battered soul who was trying his best to put on a good show, the same way she was.

She watched him lean over the pool table and execute a perfect bank shot to beat Ned. When he glanced up and caught her looking, he grinned in triumph. As she smiled back at him, the last bit of her melancholy mood disappeared. Whatever his faults, Russ had one shining virtue—he made her forget all about Tommy.

After Russ beat Steve and Ned, other challengers wandered over and Jo saw money being exchanged as cowboys started laying bets for or against Russ. Soon the half-dozen remaining customers were gathered around the pool table as the impromptu tournament continued. The excitement seemed to make folks thirsty, because drink orders increased, along with the size of tips.

Jo delivered another lemonade to Steve, who was standing on the fringe of the small crowd. "Your brother's sure good for business," she said, handing him his drink.

Steve nodded. "He's drawn a crowd all his life. Stirrin' up excitement is natural for him." He didn't sound jealous, just amused. "I hope I can get him up here to drive my sleigh when I finish restoring it. He'd pull money out of the tourists like crazy."

Jo pictured Russ in his sheepskin coat with the collar turned up and his hat pulled low over his face as he guided a horse-drawn sleigh through the snow. "I wouldn't mind a sleigh ride, myself."

He glanced at her. "I'll take you anytime you want to go. Just say the word."

She smiled and returned her attention to Russ, who'd just tilted his head back to polish off another beer before he lined up his next shot. "You're trying to keep me away from him, aren't you?"

"Yep."

"Come on, Steve. He can't be that bad. He's your brother, after all."

"Yeah, and I love the ornery cuss, warts and all. But he's hell on women. I'd hate to see him throw you off track."

"You're sweet. If I had a big brother, I'd want him to be exactly like you." She took a moment to admire the way Russ's broad shoulders stretched the material of his shirt as he reached across the table to send another ball into the pocket.

"Then take some big-brother advice. Forget that guy. He'll be on the bus back to Tucson on Sunday, anyway. I'll make sure he doesn't come in tomorrow night."

Jo felt as if someone had just snatched away a colorfully wrapped gift. "Short visit."

"That's the way he is. Stayin' in one place too long makes him nervous. Even when he's here helping me with the horseshoeing, he takes off every couple of days and spends the nights alone in the mountains, or out by Lynx Lake."

Jo understood that restlessness, all right. She'd left Montana as if her tail was on fire, and she'd felt such relief seeing nothing but new territory and new faces. Since she'd lived in Prescott, she'd taken her sleeping bag and camped out a few times at Lynx Lake, herself, searching for peace of mind.

"Maybe I have no call to stick my nose in your business," Steve said. "But you ain't got any family here to turn to, and I think if you did, they'd be telling you the same thing. Besides that, I'd hate for my own flesh and blood to be causin' you problems."

"Thanks for being so concerned about me. I—" She paused as a cowboy across the table got her attention and held up his empty glass. Turning away from the appealing sight of Russ negotiating another tricky shot, she touched Steve's shoulder. "I'll keep in mind everything you've said." Poor Steve couldn't know that the picture he'd painted made Russ even more irresistible.

When she returned to the bar, Eddie had a message for Steve. Claire's car had been making funny noises, so she and Sharon had driven home instead of staying overnight in Phoenix. They'd be pleased if their menfolk would come on home now.

Jo delivered the message to Steve and Ned as they stood watching the pool game.

"So much for boys' night out," Steve said with a grin. He didn't look particularly upset.

"I reckon this means I'll have to take Sharon back to Phoenix in the mornin'," Ned said. "She wanted me to look at a new couch, anyhow." He didn't seem perturbed by the change in plans, either.

Jo smiled at them. "Neither of you cowpokes are worth a darn as swinging bachelors, are you?"

"I guess not," Steve said. "My brother isn't gonna be happy about leavin', but I'm not giving him a choice."

As Steve went to tell Russ about the turn of events, Jo figured that was the end of her excitement for the evening. She'd had a temporary distraction from the blues, but Steve was probably right—Russ was a risky proposition, to say the least.

Steve came over to settle the bill. "Dusty wants a chance to play Russ one more time," he said. "So's he's gonna drive him back to the Double G after that."

Jo worked to hide her delight. "Oh."

"Let Dusty take him home, Jo."

She pretended to refigure the amount on Steve's tab, although she knew it was right. "Why wouldn't I?"

Steve sighed. "Why do I feel like there's gonna be a train wreck, and no matter how I throw the switches, it'll happen anyway?"

Jo handed him the bill. "You've been a good friend, warning me the way you have. But I'm twenty-seven years old, a grown woman, and if I can't take care of myself by now, there's not much hope for me."

"And you promise you'll take care of yourself?"

"I promise." She just wasn't sure what that meant right now. Maybe in the end she'd take Steve's advice and stay away from Russ. But when he looked at her, she felt a zing of anticipation that she'd almost forgotten existed. Tommy had ground down most of her sexual urges, and it was nice to discover them coming back. She wasn't ready to turn away from that good feeling—at least not quite yet.

RUSS KNEW the smart thing would have been to go home with Steve and Ned, but doing the smart thing wasn't exactly his trademark. Besides, Steve was getting a little heavy-handed with his interference, and Russ decided to stay partly to let Steve know he couldn't call the shots.

Once Steve and Ned left, Dusty ordered up another round from Jo. A couple of guys still hung around the pool table to watch, but the evening was winding down.

As Jo brought over the beers, Russ leaned on his pool cue and watched her. Damn, but she was fine to look at. He could just imagine how nice she'd be to hold, how her hair would feel when he combed his fingers through it. She took Dusty his beer before walking around the table to Russ.

"You're probably wishing we'd go home so you can close up," Russ said as he took the beer.

She shrugged, which made the hair that fell to her shoulders dance in the light. "Not really. We'd stay open another hour whether you were here or not, and Eddie's already told me I can go home anytime, now that it's so slow."

A stab of regret surprised the hell out of him. "So you're gonna leave?"

She gazed at him with those smoky eyes that fascinated him so. "I haven't decided yet."

He didn't want her to leave. He wasn't sure yet what he did want, but it wasn't to have her disappear. He dug some change out of his pocket and held it out. "While you're decidin', would you pick out a few tunes on the jukebox for me?"

"Sure." She started to take the money from his outstretched hand.

He closed his hand over hers. It was a very sweet contact indeed. "I didn't tell you what I like."

A spark flared in her eyes. "What do you like?"

"Hey, Russ, your shot," Dusty called across the table.

"Be right with you, Dusty," he said without breaking

eye contact with Jo. "Anything by Alan Jackson or Susie
Bogguss." He kept hold of her hand and stroked the
back of it lightly with his thumb.

"I like those, too. Fast songs or slow ones?"

"You choose." He loved the welcoming look that was
coming into her eyes. His heart beat a little faster. "Does
your boss let you dance with the customers?"

"Not when we're working."

He squeezed her hand and released it. "Then maybe
it's time for you to get off work," he said softly.

Her smile was a beautiful thing to see. "Maybe it is."

"Any day now, Russ," Dusty said.

"Excuse me for a minute," Russ said. "I have a little
business to take care of." He turned to the table and
quickly assessed the available shots. He'd thought about
dragging out this game a while to justify hanging
around. But the bar would be open for another hour,
and spending that hour dancing with Jo sounded a
whole lot more appealing than playing pool with Dusty.
The only hitch was that Dusty was supposed to be his
ride home, and he damned sure didn't want to walk
back to the Double G.

As one of his favorite Alan Jackson love ballads
poured out of the jukebox, he glanced at the two cowboys who'd been watching the match. "Either of you
guys plan to take on the winner of this game?"

One of them stubbed out his cigarette in an ashtray. "I
was thinkin' I might," the man said. "From the way
things've been goin', I reckon it'll be you."

"Could be."

"Hey, I can still take you, Russ," Dusty said. "I figure
you're stallin' because you're worried."

Russ sighted down his stick. "Could be."

It took longer than he'd planned to lose to Dusty. The

kid really needed to work on his game. But finally Dusty managed to put the eight ball in the pocket and swaggered over to hold out his hand to Russ.

"Hell of a game," Russ said, shaking Dusty's hand.

"You can try me again after I polish off these two."

"I'll keep that in mind." Russ wasn't worried about being called back to the table before closing time, considering the pace of Dusty's game. He'd taken so damned long to win that all the songs Russ had paid for had been played already.

Russ snapped his cue stick into the holder and picked up his half-full beer glass before crossing the room to where Jo sat on a stool talking to Eddie behind the bar. His chest tightened a notch, just looking at her. He took note of the fact and told himself to calm down. A few dances, a little bodily contact—he'd enjoyed that hundreds of times without turning it into a big deal.

He drained his glass and set it on the bar. "I need more change for the jukebox, Eddie." He dug a five out of his wallet.

Jo gave him an assessing look before she glanced back at the pool table. "You lost to Dusty?"

"'Fraid so."

Eddie laughed as he opened the cash register. "You're gonna have a hard time living that down. Nobody loses to Dusty. His game is all talk."

"Well, he put it together this time." Russ took his change and walked over to the jukebox. He picked slow songs, starting with a real mushy one by George Strait. Fast dancing was good for flirting when you had all night to play around, but he didn't have much time left. He was hungry for the feel of Jo in his arms. With George Strait singing about true love, he returned to the bar.

She glanced sideways at him, a gleam in her eye. "Ready for another beer, cowboy?"

There was that tightness in his chest again, as if something important rode on the question he was about to ask. He took a long, slow breath. "I'm here to collect a dance, if you're so inclined."

Jo turned to Eddie. "I'm officially off duty, right?"

"Yep. Go enjoy yourself. We don't have what you'd call a rush of business at the moment."

Jo laid her hat on the bar and slid off the stool.

"Then let's dance." She walked to the tiny dance floor, turned and held out her arms.

He made the mistake of looking into her eyes as he gathered her in, and he couldn't seem to look away again. The sweetness of her body against his almost made him moan out loud, and his system started going haywire as they moved with the music. *This is no big deal,* he reminded himself again, trying desperately to believe it. Dear God, but Jo felt good cuddled up against him like this.

"Steve says you like to camp out at Lynx Lake sometimes," she said.

"And what else did my big brother have to say about me?" He trusted Steve not to blab stories Russ had specifically asked him not to, but that still left a lot for Steve to talk about.

"He said you were hell on women."

"Is that right?" Russ lost himself in the softness of her gaze. "And did you believe him?"

"Well, Steve isn't the kind to lie, so I suppose I should believe him."

"Then what are you doin' here, sweetheart? Why aren't you headed for home as fast as you can go?"

"I figured a dance or two wouldn't hurt anything. I like to dance."

"So do I." He tightened his hold on her and watched the flame in her eyes grow brighter. If Steve knew the ideas that were coming to his mind, he'd likely want to horsewhip him. "How come you moved all the way down here from Montana?"

"How come you never stay in one place very long?"

He smiled, recognizing himself in her. That's just how he liked to answer a personal question, by turning it right back. "Maybe I like seeing different scenery."

"Maybe I do, too."

He liked her spirit. He could imagine how that spirit would spice up a session in bed, not that he planned to find out.

That tightness in his chest was back, though, as if something was about to happen. "You sure have improved the scenery around this place," he said.

Her cheeks grew pink, but she didn't look away, as some women did when he gave them a compliment. She kept gazing right up at him. "I could say the same, cowboy."

Heat surged through him. "Oh, lady, you're playin' with fire, here."

"But playing it safe isn't much fun."

"You got that right." The song ended and they stood still, gazing into each other's eyes. He was afraid if he stood like that too much longer he might kiss her, and he had no intention of doing that in front of Eddie and three nosey cowboys.

As the next ballad started, he cupped his hand around her head and nestled her cheek against his chest. "That's enough talkin'. Let's just dance a while."

"Mmm." She snuggled against him.

He wondered if she could hear the pounding of his heart and if she knew how much she was affecting him. Something was different about this woman. He didn't usually go off the deep end so fast. In fact, he was having a hard time remembering if he'd ever gone this crazy over simple flirting and a couple of dances.

It wasn't the booze. He'd been so busy playing pool he hadn't had much time to get serious about drinking. Some of this might be Steve's fault. If Steve hadn't told him to stay away from Jo, maybe he wouldn't have been so interested in getting a little closer. But being ticked off at Steve didn't explain this pull he felt every time he looked into her eyes. It didn't explain the way she fit into his arms as if the two of them were connecting pieces of a puzzle.

The top of her head was just the right height for him to lay his cheek against her hair, and he gave in to the temptation. Her hair was soft as silk and smelled like flowers. He closed his eyes. No use trying to figure it out. Some things in life were beyond his understanding, and this perfect moment of dancing with a girl he'd never seen before tonight was one of them.

They covered less and less dance floor as Russ was happy just to sway to the music holding this warm, sweet-smelling woman close in his arms. He kept moving with her even during the gaps between songs, as if the two if them had established a rhythm that didn't depend on the tunes coming from the jukebox.

The pressure of her body against his created an ache in his groin that was persistent but manageable, so long as he didn't look into her eyes again, so long as he couldn't hear the gentle temptation of her voice. Steve was right. This woman was far too good for the likes of him. But for the time being, he could warm his soul and ease his pain, letting the blackness that followed him everywhere gradually drift away.

Then somebody tapped him on the shoulder and the magic evaporated.

With murder in his heart, he raised his head and opened his eyes to find Dusty standing next to them. He focused his best narrow-eyed glare on the man. "Son, I hope for your sake the building's burnin' down."

Dusty looked nervous, but he held his ground. "My pool game's gone cold. I'm ready to leave."

Jo stiffened in his arms, and he rubbed a soothing hand over her back. "Give me a minute, Dusty. I'm dancing with the lady."

"After this song, then."

Russ clenched his jaw. Most of the time he was relieved not to have a driver's license, but needing to hitch a ride with arrogant pups like Dusty didn't sit well with him. He gave Dusty a brief nod and turned Jo so that his back was toward the lanky young cowboy. With a sigh he settled his cheek against Jo's hair again and closed his eyes.

Jo tightened her grip on him and murmured something, but it was muffled against his chest.

Russ leaned down so his ear was closer. "What did you say, little darlin'?"

"I don't want you to go."

His heart slammed against his ribs and he wondered if she knew what she was saying. "I don't want to go, either. But Dusty's my ride home."

She lifted her head and her mouth was kissing close.

"I could give you a ride."

He looked into those green, green eyes. Being a good guy was getting tougher by the minute. "I have no doubt of that, sweetheart. But my brother's right. I'm not the type for you to get tangled up with. I'd best go with Dusty."

"Is that what you want?" she said.

He closed his eyes and tried to hold on to some sense of honor. "You don't need to be considerin' what I want."

"Then I'll tell you what I want," she said quietly. "I'm feeling alive again for the first time in ages, and I need that feeling just for a little while longer. Right or wrong, I can't be alone tonight."

Opening his eyes, he faced the need shining from hers. It was a perfect match to the need in his heart. "I can't make you any promises."

"I'm not asking for any."

He hesitated, wondering if he'd burn in hell for giving this woman what she wanted tonight when he knew that was all he'd ever be able to give her.

"Go tell Dusty you have a ride home," she whispered.

Come to think of it, he'd probably burn in hell anyway. One more sin wouldn't make much difference. "All right."

3

WHAT THEY WERE about to do was wild and irresponsible, Jo thought as she and Russ climbed into her old truck. Well, not totally irresponsible. Russ had made a stop in the men's room before they left the Roundup and Jo knew good and well what he'd been after.

She was scared, no doubt about it, but still absolutely certain that she'd regret it for the rest of her life if she didn't spend this night with Russ. He made her feel desirable again, and she hadn't realized how much she needed that.

Maybe it took somebody like Russ, a man with his own secret sorrows, to ease the pain in her heart. Dancing with him had been heaven, and she could only think of one thing that would be better than that. She deserved to know what that other pleasure was like.

But risking this much made her nervous, and she ground the gears on her truck while backing out of the parking space. Then she killed the engine by forgetting to shift into first at a stoplight. Her Alan Jackson tape in the cassette player sputtered to a stop when the engine died, and when the heater didn't work right she discovered she'd switched on the air conditioner instead.

"You don't do this much, do you?" Russ asked.

She tried to calm herself as she twisted the key in the ignition, got the truck going again and turned on the heater. "Shoot, I've been driving a stick since I was twelve," she said. "Old Bessie probably needs a tune-up."

"I wasn't talking about driving."

Jo sighed. He seemed to see through her so easily that she might as well be honest about her lack of experience.

"No, I don't do this much."

"You can still change your mind."

She took a deep breath that was filled with the scent of leather, after-shave and aroused male. "I don't want to change my mind."

"Then maybe you oughta switch on your headlights."

With a groan she pulled out the knob for the truck's lights. "Real smooth, huh?"

There was a smile in his voice. "I'm not complainin', sweetheart."

Her pulse lurched. She wasn't very experienced at this, but he was. When she got him inside her apartment, she could relax and let him take the lead. The thought made her dizzy and the engine bucked as she forgot to shift...again.

Russ steadied himself against the dashboard. "Although I do hope you don't live far away."

"No, not far." Alan Jackson's song filled the silence. "I guess it was fate that Dusty beat you in pool."

His low laughter rumbled in the darkness. "Fate might've brought me into the Roundup tonight, but fate had nothin' to do with losing that game."

Warmth spread through her. "You lost on purpose?"

"Yep."

"Goodness. Dusty will be bragging about that for weeks. I can't believe you ruined your reputation as a great pool player because of me." His lack of ego added another layer to his considerable appeal.

"I had a hankerin' for a dance or two." He paused.

"But I want you to know I didn't plan this part. I was going to walk away."

"I know you were. I—" *I'm the one who begged you to stay with me.* "I'll take responsibility for changing your mind. With Steve, I mean, if he—"

"Don't worry about Steve," he said gently. "I'll handle him."

"I don't want Steve to think you took advantage of me."

"Well, now, little darlin', you may not be able to do anything about the way Steve thinks. Knowing him, he'll figure I had this in mind from the first time I saw you."

"But you didn't."

"That's not entirely true, either." His voice stroked her like a caress. "I just thought I'd be strong enough to resist you. Turns out I'm not."

She let out a long breath. "Thank you for that. I don't think I could have survived another rejection tonight."

"Another one?"

Damn. That had slipped out. Now she'd have to offer some explanation or he'd think she'd propositioned somebody else before he came along. "I didn't mean I'd been rejected tonight. It was a year ago tonight, and it's...been on my mind. But that's all I want to say about the subject, if that's okay."

"Sweetheart, you don't have to talk about a blessed thing you don't want to. I have a few things I don't like draggin' out in the open, myself."

He understood, as she'd sensed he would. He could give her what she needed without questioning why, because he hungered in the same way. For this night, they would bring comfort to each other. She wouldn't think beyond that.

As she turned down her street, she decided not to bother hauling up the garage door and putting the truck inside. She'd be driving him home again in the morning, anyway. Oh, God. She was trembling with excitement and anxiety.

"No roommate?" he asked as they walked up to her front door.

"No. I like my space."

"Me, too."

After a couple of tries she got her key into the lock and in short order they were inside, with the door locked behind them. The lamp she always left on filled the small living room with a soft glow.

He looked around. "Looks real nice."

She gazed at him, barely able to believe this was happening. She'd never brought home a guy she'd just met. Never. "Can I...take your coat?"

He took it off and laid it across the back of the rocking chair. "That's good enough." Then he removed his hat and hung it on the chair arm. "Maybe I can take your coat."

She held her breath as he came close and slipped the heavy wool coat from her shoulders. She looked into his eyes, dark as midnight, and her heart pumped fire through her veins.

"There's all kinds of ways to forget what we don't want to remember," he murmured. "I reckon I've tried 'em all. But this here's one of my favorites." Taking his time, he reached up and stroked his knuckles lightly from her throat to the plunging neckline of her blouse.

She gasped as a spasm of reaction rippled deep within her.

"It's been a while for you, hasn't it, sweetheart?"

She nodded. She had no desire to remember that last time with Tommy.

"That'll make my job real easy, then." He popped the first pearl snap on her low-cut blouse. "Nothin' better than making love to a gal who's been saving up."

Moisture pooled in her mouth as he popped the next snap, then the next. She swallowed. "Should we...go into the bedroom?"

"Not yet, sweet thing." He finished with her blouse and reached for the front catch of her bra. "There's a lot we can get done right here. And I like the light." He flicked her bra open with a practiced hand and gently moved the material aside as his gaze lowered. "Now, if that ain't a mighty fine sight."

She trembled as he cupped her breast in his work-roughened hand.

"God didn't make anything prettier or nicer to touch than a woman's breast." He brushed his thumb lazily back and forth across her nipple.

She closed her eyes and wondered if she'd have her first orgasm while they stood right here, his hand caressing her breast.

"Ah, sweetheart, you're shaking already, aren't you?"

She opened her eyes and looked up. Never in her life had she felt so vulnerable. Never had a man brought her to the brink with just the look in his eyes and the casual stroke of his thumb.

His warm smile and soft voice flowed over her.

"Don't be scared. It's good to want someone like this. Some folks never let themselves."

She swallowed. "Do...you?"

"I sure do. Right this minute I do. I'm fixin' to wear you out." He slid his arm around her. "Arch your back, darlin'." He leaned down and urged her breast closer to his mouth. "Let's see if you taste as nice as you feel."

As he took her in his hot mouth, the moist tug of his lips and tongue arrowed straight to her core.

"Mmm," he murmured. "Doggone if you don't taste even better." Cradling her breast in his hand, bringing her hips tight against his, he settled in.

She gripped his shoulders as the rhythmic suction of his mouth sent an urgent signal to her trembling center. She couldn't possibly be coming apart this fast...but she was. A small cry escaped her and she held on for dear life as she began to shudder and gasp in his arms.

The wave of her climax splashed her with such force that she didn't realize he'd unfastened her shorts until he slipped his hand inside her panties. He probed deep, synchronizing his strokes to the tremors rocking her. Before the first explosion was spent he urged her upward again, finding her other breast with his mouth, seeking her passion-drenched channel with his knowing touch.

She began to pant, and this time, when he flung her over the edge, her small cry became a lusty groan of delight. He kept his fingers moving within her until the last quiver subsided. Then slowly, gently, he withdrew his hand, sliding it over her belly and up the valley between her breasts. When he cupped her chin in that same hand, the scent of her unbridled response wafted between them, tightening the knot of desire in her once again.

He gazed into her eyes. "Now that your motor's running, it's time for that trip to the bedroom."

She took a deep breath. "I can't. My bones have melted."

His grin was pure male. "Now, I do like hearing that."

"It's true. If you let go, I'll slide right down to the floor."

"But I'm not lettin' go, honey. We've got a whole lot of night left."

She looked up at him, her senses dazed by the possibilities. "I still have my boots on."

"That's a fact."

"I've never...had that happen while my boots were still on."

"It happened twice," he reminded her with a twinkle in his eyes.

"So it did," she murmured. "And you haven't even kissed me yet."

"We'll get to that." He swung her limp body into his arms and walked toward the bedroom. "Later."

"If I didn't know better, I'd think you were a tease."

"That's just what I am." He laid her on the bed and switched on the lamp. "And I love teasing pretty ladies like you." Sitting beside her on the bed, he pulled off his boots before turning to hers. After her boots hit the floor, he peeled off one sock and began to massage her foot.

"Mmm, that's not teasing. That just feels nice." She was as relaxed as a rag doll, everywhere except at the moist place between her thighs, which began to pulse, even from something as innocent as a foot massage.

"'Course it feels nice. You've been on your feet for hours." He slid off the other sock and began to rub her other foot. "Ticklish?"

"No." She lay there in total abandon, her clothes unfastened, most of her body revealed in the lamplight.

"Then just hold still." He brought her foot to his mouth and slipped his tongue into the crevice behind her toes.

She gasped at the sensuous glide of his tongue as he

pushed it between each of her toes. She'd never imagined the space between her toes was an erogenous zone, but with this man, every inch of her was fast turning into one. She moaned as a now-familiar ache began to build. He massaged her calves and sucked gently on her toes until her breathing grew ragged. Oh, he was a tease, all right. She reached for her shorts, meaning to push them out of the way.

"Let me, little darlin'." Still ministering to her right foot, he bent her left knee and pulled her shorts and panties off on one side.

"I want—"

"Let me guess."

Before she quite knew how it happened, he'd slipped down on the bed, hooked her knees over his shoulders, and claimed the most intimate caress of all.

"Good...guess," she whispered. Oh, Lordy, the man was an artist. He'd coax her up the slope, then pause just shy of the top to let her tumble partway down again. After several rounds of that game, she begged for release. When he gave it, she celebrated with heartfelt cries of completion.

As she lay spent and gasping, he slowly nuzzled his way up her dew-slicked body and settled his mouth over hers. The effect was stunning. As she tasted his lips for the first time, as she accepted the first thrust of his tongue, the salty tang of her own passion flavored their first-ever kiss.

He kissed her with deep thoroughness, as if to brand the moment into her mind forever. Then he lifted his head. "Don't go away."

She gave him a lazy smile. "Couldn't. I think you've nailed me to the bed."

"Nope. That comes next."

He undressed with economical movements and without a speck of vanity. He had a right to be vain if he'd wanted to, she thought. Except for a ragged purple scar on his chest, a scar nearly covered by dark, curly hair, he was perfect. The strong upper body of a professional blacksmith narrowed to the slim hips of a seasoned cowboy. He was solidly aroused, and without embarrassment he took a condom out of his jeans pocket and put it on.

When the task was finished, he glanced at her. "Think that'll do?"

"Come here and let's find out." She'd never met a man so easy with his sexuality and hers, a man who openly enjoyed every moment in the joining of a man and woman. This was a cowboy who'd wake up next to you in the morning and want to start right in again. Good thing she didn't have classes she'd have to cut tomorrow. Maybe she could find someone to work her shift at the Roundup, too. Steve had said Russ was leaving on Sunday. If she had her way, he wouldn't leave her bed until then.

Russ HAD SERIOUSLY miscalculated. He'd figured on having a good time tonight, but he hadn't figured on losing his mind and going plum crazy over the woman. Jo was sweeter and more ready for love than he'd imagined in his wildest dreams, and doggone if he wasn't getting ideas he had no right having.

He'd be better off leaving now, but he wasn't strong enough to go without sinking into her heat at least once. He desperately needed to relieve the ache he'd been nursing ever since they left the bar, and he didn't know many men who could turn away from the sight of Jo lying there with her clothes mostly off and heaven in her smoky green eyes. It was a dangerous business, though, climbing into her bed and wondering if he'd have the good sense to climb out again when the party was over.

He gazed down at her, knowing this picture would stay with him a long time. "Whoever undressed you didn't do much of a job."

"That's your opinion." Her voice was bedroom low, rich with the love they'd been making and the love yet to make.

He put his knee on the bed and eased away the shorts and panties still wound around her creamy thigh. "For the next little while, I don't want nothin' between your legs but me."

"I'd say that's more than enough, cowboy."

He moved over her and faced the fact he was trembling with need. That wasn't good. He'd hold off a while and prove to himself he was still in control of the situation. As he gazed into her eyes, a sinking sensation in the pit of his stomach warned that he was in bigger trouble than he'd thought.

She lifted her soft hands and cupped his face. God help him, he loved her gentle touch, loved the look in her eyes, all hot and eager for what was to come. He turned his head and kissed her palm. Then he kissed his way down the inside of her arm, his pulse hammering as he moved across her shoulder and finally took her mouth with his.

A kiss wasn't supposed to be like this, he thought. It was only a means to an end, not an end itself. But he didn't remember any woman's mouth fitting quite so perfectly as Jo's, or being quite as soft, or tasting quite as good. He could get addicted to kissing her. He forced himself to lift his head and end the kiss, but then her lashes fluttered open, and there he was looking into the flames again.

She slid her hands down his back and took hold of his hips. Her slow smile was the sexiest thing he'd ever seen. "I think you promised—" She urged him closer and arched upward. "—to nail me to the bed."

With a groan he gave up his sanity and slid in deep. His chest tightened and his eyes burned as he realized that this was it. Damned if this feeling wasn't exactly what love songs were all about. He'd decided the songs were just make-believe, because in all the times he'd been inside a woman, he'd never known this rightness, this sense of coming home. But he was there now, no matter how little he deserved to be. With luck, what was going on inside him was purely one-sided, and Jo felt nothing but physical enjoyment.

He closed his eyes and concentrated on giving her exactly that. Afterward, he'd get the hell out of her life before he started expecting things he had no right to.

"I like it when you look at me," she murmured.

He liked that, too. Way too much. Reluctantly, aware of the risk to his heart, he opened his eyes as he moved slowly within her.

Her gaze was soft and her lips parted as she took in quick, shallow breaths. He kissed her again. Couldn't help it. Couldn't help any of the emotions tumbling around in his chest as his mouth absorbed her low moan of pleasure.

As he continued to kiss her, he maintained a steady rhythm designed to make her climax, and he used every mental trick in the book to keep from exploding first. If this was the first and last time he'd love her like this, he wanted it to be damn near perfect. He quivered from the effort, and their bodies grew slippery with sweat. Bury-

ing himself again and again in her warmth, he felt at last
the tightening as she dug her fingers into his back. He
lifted his lips from hers to watch her eyes darken and her
cheeks flush.

"Oh...Russ."

The sound of his name, spoken almost with reverence,
went through him like a bolt of lightning. He'd never
known such joy while giving a woman pleasure. Words,
crazy words, spun through his mind, but he had just
enough control left to hold them back. "Enjoyin' yourself, darlin'?" He'd deliberately avoided calling her by
name all evening. It was his way of keeping his distance
and making the women blend together.

"Yes...yes!" Her eyes grew wide as she arched upward, abandoning herself to the wildness deep inside.

That did it. He poured himself into her in the most
shattering orgasm of his life. And dimly he heard himself groan out the name he'd been so careful not to say.
Jo.

JO AWOKE in the darkened bedroom, aware that Russ's
arms were no longer around her as they had been when
she'd drifted into a satisfied, deep sleep. In fact, he
wasn't in the bed anymore. The luminous dial on the
nightstand clock said it was almost three in the morning.

She lay still and listened for any indication he was still
in the apartment. The total quiet suggested he was gone.
His clothes were no longer scattered over her bedroom
floor, and the living-room light they'd left burning was
turned off. But she was so unwilling to believe that he'd
abandon her without a word that she got up, wrapped
the quilt from the bed around her and started a search.

Nothing. Not even a note. She couldn't believe it. A
man who treated a woman with such tenderness and

passion had to be more sensitive than to leave her in the middle of the night without a word. She'd looked into his eyes when they'd made love and she'd seen the caring expression there. And most of all, she'd heard the emotion he'd poured into saying her name when he'd finally given himself up to a climax.

She hadn't expected him to pledge undying love. That was exactly the sort of awkwardness she hadn't wanted and the reason she'd instinctively been drawn to a man like Russ. Neither of them had been looking to start a committed relationship on the basis of one night of passion.

But she had expected him to stick around for breakfast. He had no transportation, either, so he'd either hitched or walked back to the ranch. Walked, most likely, considering not many people would be out driving around in the middle of the night picking up hitchhikers. Cowboys hated few things more than hoofing it. He must have been mighty eager to get home if he'd walked the distance from her apartment to the ranch.

Wandering back into the bedroom, Jo flopped onto the mattress and stared at the ceiling. Nothing made sense. He'd been more than willing to spend the night with her, and he didn't seem like the type who lost interest the minute he'd scored. They'd had a memorable time, one that she'd hoped might be extended a little longer. She hadn't scared him off with talk about love everlasting, so what the hell was his problem?

She'd find out, somehow. She'd have to swallow her pride to question Steve about his brother's whereabouts, but her pride wasn't in wonderful shape at the moment, anyway. Doggone it. She swallowed a lump in her throat. In trying to erase a bad memory from this particular night, she'd gone and made things worse.

4

EARLY THE NEXT MORNING Russ followed the steady sound of a pitchfork tossing straw out of a stall and found Steve working in the barn.

Steve glanced up. "Well, did you take some of the brag out of Dusty last night?"

Russ hated what was coming, but it was time to pay up for what he'd done. "I let him win."

Steve stopped mucking out the stall and leaned on the pitchfork. "You don't say?" His eyes narrowed in speculation. "That must have been a painful ride home, listening to him carry on," he said slowly.

Russ held his ground and met his brother's stare.

"You might as well hear this from me as from someone else. I didn't ride home with Dusty. I went home with Jo."

Steve gazed at him in silence. Finally he shoved his hat back and sighed. "I shoulda never left you there."

"Probably not."

"I didn't hear no truck this mornin'. How'd you get home?"

"Walked."

Steve tossed the pitchfork down and clenched his fists. "You *walked?* What in hell did you do that made her mad enough to let you walk home?"

"She wasn't mad, at least not when I left. She was asleep."

"Good God. You snuck out on her?"

Russ welcomed Steve's anger. He deserved it, considering how Jo must be feeling this morning. "You were right about her, big brother. She's one terrific lady. Leavin' her was one of the hardest things I've ever done in my life, but I had to."

"I want to know why you had to go home with her in the first place. You shoulda known it would turn out like this."

Guilt hammered him. "It was stupid, but that's no surprise, coming from me. I thought I could just have a good time with her, and I didn't realize... The thing is, she seemed to need...oh, hell, never mind. I called Ned just now. I'm catching a ride to Phoenix with him and Sharon and I'll get a bus from there."

"Just like that. No explanation to Jo."

Russ clenched his jaw. "There's only one thing I could tell her, and I don't plan to get into all that. So the only solution is to disappear. Better to hurt her a little bit now instead of making things worse later."

"Oh, I get it. You think what happened with Sarah gives you the right to act like a smelly pile of cow chips."

"No, dammit." He jammed his hands into the pockets of his jacket. "What happened with Sarah gives me no rights at all when it comes to a woman like Jo. Jo is the most loving, kind, sweet..." He sputtered to a stop, knowing he'd said way too much.

Steve's expression softened a little. "She got to you, didn't she?"

Russ could face Steve's anger this morning, but not his kindness. He turned away.

"Don't leave today, little brother. Let me drive you back to Jo's house. Talk this thing out. Tell her about the devils chasin' you."

"No way."

"Look, you've got this thing all twisted up in your head. What happened with Sarah was terrible. But closin' yourself off from life and thinking you can't ever get serious about another woman ain't gonna make it right again. It's the worst thing you can do, if you want to know."

Russ swung back to him. "Oh, that's real easy for you to say! You weren't on that road to Cloudcroft, now, were you? You didn't see what your little brother did to a beautiful, loving, innocent young woman!"

Steve regarded him quietly. "No, I wasn't there. But I'm here to see what you're doin' to yourself, and it's a sin. Somebody like Jo Cassidy just might be able to drag you back from that hell you live in, if you'd give her a chance."

A wave of longing washed over him, but he let it pass before he spoke again. "It's not happening. I'm going to do Jo a favor and never see her again. I'd appreciate it if you'd tell Claire goodbye for me. If I know Claire, she'll be full of questions I don't want to answer."

"What do you want me to tell Jo? You know she's gonna ask about you the next time I go to the Roundup."

Russ hadn't thought about that. "You're not going to say anything about Sarah, are you?"

"I promised you I wouldn't the day you came back from New Mexico. That promise still stands."

"Then tell her..." He paused and cursed softly to himself. Anything he really wanted to say to soothe the hurt he'd caused would only give her hope. And there was no hope. "Don't tell her anything. Just say your no-account brother took off, and it's a good thing for her that he did. You can go on like that all you want. You know the drill."

Steve pulled his hat back down over his eyes and picked up the pitchfork. "You comin' back for Christmas? Claire would sure like it if you would."

"You don't need me around at Christmas."

"You never know." Steve's tone was casual as he shoved the pitchfork into the straw. "Then again, you might need us."

"The only thing I need at Christmas is a bottle of tequila and a shot glass."

"You've tried that, and I'll bet all you ended up with was a hat that was a size too small the next mornin'. Why not give a family Christmas a chance this year?"

"Don't plan on it."

"Just remember, the invitation stands."

"Thanks." Russ headed out of the barn, but he turned back at the door. "And thanks for...for puttin' up with me."

"You're my brother. Simple as that."

Russ left the barn, a lump in his throat. He wished he could be as good a brother to Steve as Steve was to him.

Somebody like Steve was the kind of guy Jo deserved. With luck, she'd find a good man and forget all about last night. Unfortunately for him, last night would probably stay with him forever.

THAT NIGHT at the Roundup Jo glanced nervously at the door each time a new group of cowboys came in. Finally, Steve showed up, followed closely by Ned. Jo's heart beat faster as she anticipated seeing Russ amble in after Ned. After all, he wasn't scheduled to leave until Sunday. She was prepared for him to appear as if nothing had happened, joking and laughing as if he hadn't pulled a cowardly disappearing act after getting up close and really personal with her. She wouldn't let him get away with that for a minute.

He didn't come in joking and laughing. He didn't come in at all.

Jo's first panicked thought that something had happened to Russ evaporated as she took note of Steve and Ned's behavior. If something terrible had happened, Steve and Ned wouldn't be acting so normal. In fact, they wouldn't be in here having a drink at all.

Grabbing a tray, she forced herself not to hurry as she went to their table. "Evening, gentlemen. A couple of the usual?"

Steve glanced up at her with a wary smile. "That'd be fine, Jo."

A hollow feeling grew in the pit of her stomach. "I guess Russ must be busy tonight."

Steve looked unhappy. "I'm sorry, Jo. Russ left for Tucson this mornin'."

Gone. She should have been prepared for it, but she wasn't. The news hurt and hurt bad.

"I'm the varmint who drove him down to catch the bus in Phoenix," Ned said, looking equally miserable. "If I'da knowed what he was up to, I wouldn't've taken him."

She tried to believe this wasn't as bad as it seemed. "Did he...give you any message for me?"

Steve cleared his throat. "No. Sorry."

She was surprised at how much pain landed on her heart. She hadn't been looking for more than an exciting evening to take her mind off Tommy, so it made no sense to be upset. But she kept remembering the tender expression on Russ's face as he'd moved deep inside her. She remembered the look in his eyes, as if she meant a lot more to him than one night of sexual release. Apparently she'd put too much importance on that look. It seemed Russ Gibson had an angel's touch and a devil's soul.

Steve put his hand on her arm. "Listen, Jo, I love my brother, but he's treatin' you terrible. I figured this could happen, although I always hold out the hope that someday... Anyway, it's not you that's the problem. It's him. He...scares real easy."

Her jaw tensed as anger replaced hurt. "I did absolutely nothing to scare him. I'm not looking to tie somebody down, or make demands. So, as far as I'm concerned, he and his precious fears can taking a flying leap." My God, she was blinking back tears. This was terrible. Russ was nothing to her. Nothing at all. "I'll get you your drinks," she said quickly, turning away.

Steve caught her arm. "Look, I'll go down to Tucson and drag his sorry ass back here so he can apologize for being a jerk."

"Yeah, and I'll help you," Ned added. "He shouldn't have gone off like that, leaving you to wonder what's goin' on. It ain't right."

"Please don't go after him," she said. "If that's the way he wants things to be between us, that's how they'll be. I've never chased after a man in my life and I'm not fixing to do it now."

Steve squeezed her arm. "I'm sorry, Jo. Sorrier than I can say."

"Hey, it's not your fault, Steve," she said. "You tried to keep this from happening, but we're both full-grown and allowed to mess up on our own. But if that brother of yours didn't have any message for me, I have one for him, whenever you talk to him again. Tell him..." She paused, thinking of just what sentiments she wanted to leave Russ with, considering how he'd dumped her in the mud and walked away. "Tell him he was...passable, for an Arizona boy."

Ned winced. "He ain't gonna like that."

"Too bad." Jo gazed at Steve. "Will you tell him that for me?"

"I've a mind to tell him a whole lot more."

"No, I'd appreciate it if you wouldn't. Just give him that message. That's the best you can do for me."

Steve nodded. "Okay. It's your call."

JO SPENT most of her waking hours for the next few days thinking about Russ. If only he'd been a lousy lover. Even an average lover would have been easy to forget after the way he'd treated her. But he'd been the best she'd ever known, and if he showed up at the Roundup again, if he smiled that knowing smile and asked her to take him home with her, she might swallow her pride and do it.

Most likely he was the kind of man who enjoyed keeping a woman off balance so she never knew what to expect from him. Considering the exams Jo had coming up, that would be the worst kind of man to have around. It would be another case of a cowboy bushwhacking her ambitions, and she couldn't face herself or her folks if she allowed that to happen a second time.

After all, she'd left Montana to get away from a man like that, so she'd look like some sort of fool if she hooked right up with another one.

But she knew her weaknesses. Russ would be able to get past her resolve if he tried hard enough. Shoot, after the way he'd made love to her, he wouldn't even have to try all that hard. He could just shove that Stetson back on his head, give her a wink and crook his finger. She needed a strategy, and she needed it in place before Russ showed up again, or she'd be kissing her education goodbye the minute she kissed that cowboy hello.

She woke up one morning with the perfect answer. She hurried to her jewelry box. Sure enough, buried under a pile of junk jewelry was the wedding band she'd taken off her finger a year ago. She'd always meant to sell it, or melt it down and turn it into something useful, like a gold paper clip to hold her divorce papers together. She slipped it on the ring finger of her left hand. Next time Russ came into the Roundup, Josephine Abigail Cassidy would be a married woman.

ONE THING Jo could say for the cowboys who frequented the Roundup Saloon—they respected the bonds of holy matrimony. As soon as she announced her marriage, the tone of her conversations with every man in the place changed. Oh, they'd still kid with her, still leave nice tips, but that spark of interest she'd noticed in more than one gaze since she'd started waitressing was gone.

With no social life, she had tons of study time. She made the dean's list with room to spare, and another semester like this might earn her a scholarship. But as the Christmas holidays loomed, she began to feel very sorry for herself.

She'd strung barbed wire to keep Russ out, and inside that corral she was one lonesome filly. All her college friends and waitress buddies thought she was a newlywed, and keeping up that fiction meant she couldn't risk a close friendship with any of them. Going back to Montana to see her folks for the day or two she could spare from work wasn't really possible on her tight budget, and the way her luck was going, she'd probably run into Tommy.

She volunteered to work Christmas Eve to enjoy the holiday atmosphere and human contact for a little longer before facing Christmas alone. For the holidays Eddie had splurged on Santa's-helper outfits for the waitresses and decorated the bar with pine wreaths and big red bows. Dressed in a short skirt of red velvet trimmed in white fur, a snug red velvet top and a Santa hat, Jo felt a little more in the spirit of the season as she moved through the jovial crowd.

She wondered if there was any chance Russ and Steve might walk in, although Steve might be too busy getting ready to play Santa, and she knew Russ wasn't big on Christmas. She didn't want to see Russ, not really. But she'd thought she'd have at least one chance to flaunt her wedding ring in his face. He hadn't shown up at the Roundup since that Friday after Thanksgiving.

Jo gave up on seeing either of the Gibson brothers when Ned arrived alone and walked over to sit with the Bascomb brothers. Ned hadn't spent many evenings at the Roundup since his wedding two weeks ago, and Jo certainly hadn't expected to see him tonight.

"Don't tell me you had a spat with Sharon on Christmas Eve," she said, serving Ned a beer.

"Just the opposite. I've been coming in here for a Christmas Eve drink ever since I was legal, and she insisted I keep it up—didn't want to ruin none of my traditions." He lowered his voice and leaned closer to Jo. "But the real reason is she plans to be waitin' in some sexy nightgown when I get home. She needs some time alone to set the scene with candles and such."

"How sweet, Ned." A pang of longing shot through Jo. Christmas was a wonderful time to be in love. It seemed so long since... A picture of Russ flashed through her mind. But that wasn't love. That was...she didn't really know what it had been except a huge mistake.

"Reckon you'll be spending Christmas with your husband."

"What?" Jo pulled herself out of her mental fog.

"Your new hubby. I didn't think you'd be here tonight. Thought you'd be home with him."

"Oh. He's...he'll be coming in later."

"He'd better not be comin' in too much later. This snowstorm's liable to make travel real difficult."

"I'm sure everything will be fine." For a moment Jo allowed herself to fantasize about how nice it would be to have a man coming home to her this Christmas Eve. Unfortunately, the man in her fantasy bore a strong resemblance to Russ. "You and Sharon have a merry Christmas," she said, squeezing his shoulder.

"Same to you, Jo. And to—doggone, I keep forgetting your husband's name."

Jo had a hard time remembering it, herself. "Ronald," she replied, hoping that was the same name she'd given out last time the question came up.

"Boy, my brain must be turning to mush. I was about to say it was Richard."

Richard. That was it, not Ronald. Damn. "Oh, Ronald's his middle name, so I call him that sometimes, just for fun."

"He must hate them two names together. Richard Ronald."

"I'm sure he does. Well, gotta get back to work, Ned. Drive careful on those snowy roads, you hear?"

Not long afterward, Jo had to take her own advice as she inched home, the chains on her truck tires jingling and crunching on the snow-packed roads. The bar had closed early due to the storm that had turned Prescott into a winter wonderland. People said they couldn't remember ever having this much snow on Christmas Eve. Jo hoped Steve and Claire would be extra cautious making their rounds tonight.

She turned up the heat on the old truck and wrapped her wool coat around her bare legs as she drove. Inside the warmth of the bar, the skimpy red velvet skirt had worked out just fine, but she should have brought along some leggings for the drive home. When she got to her duplex, she'd climb into her favorite sweats, make hot chocolate and settle in with *It's a Wonderful Life.* Her family had watched that movie every Christmas Eve since she could remember. Her mom had sent her a copy as an early gift, considering she couldn't be home for the holidays.

Pulling the truck into the garage, she wrestled the door down and hurried through the connecting one into the kitchen. In no time she'd switched on the Christmas-tree lights, punched the button on her CD player so Clint Black could sing her a few carols and headed into the bedroom to change clothes. By God, she was going to do Christmas up right, even if she had to whip up the cheer all by herself.

Just as she finished hanging up her coat and was about to take the Santa hat off, the doorbell rang. Her first thought was that Steve and Claire had delivered the kittens to Lucile and spilled the beans about who'd come up with the idea. She hoped her neighbor wasn't angry with her. The poor woman had said no cat could ever replace her Pookie, so she might as well have nothing. But Jo thought one look at two little bundles of fur would change all that in a hurry.

She decided to leave the Santa hat on because it would make Lucile laugh. In fact, she'd invite Lucile and the kittens inside to watch *It's a Wonderful Life*. She should have thought of it sooner. Lucile was special for another reason—living right next door she'd have been hard to fool, so Jo had trusted her with the knowledge that her marriage was a fake.

Jo opened her door with a grin on her face and nearly toppled backward in surprise. Russ stood on her front stoop. Under the shadow of his Stetson his cheeks glowed pink from the cold, and he wore his heavy sheepskin jacket with the collar turned up.

Jo blinked, wondering if she'd fallen asleep in front of the television and was dreaming that Russ was here. Either that or she'd been a fool to stop believing in Santa Claus.

5

"SORRY TO DISTURB your Christmas," Russ said. "I didn't know what else to do. Your neighbor won't let me in the house. She thinks I'm drunk. I wonder if you could—"

"Why do you need to get into Lucile's house?"

"Because I—ouch." He winced and clutched at his jacket. Something was squirming beneath it.

"What's under your jacket?"

"Kittens." He glanced at a water-stained list in his free hand. "Your neighbor is the one who's supposed to get 'em, right?"

Understanding dawned, although she still found the whole thing hard to believe. "You're helping Steve, aren't you?"

"Appears so."

"Did you divide up the job with Steve and Claire?"

"Nope. I'm the whole show. Steve and Claire took sick yesterday. Flu or something. I came up from Tucson to help out, because they didn't have anybody else they could call to take over, and the presents have to get delivered." He winced again as a muffled squeak came from beneath his jacket.

"Come inside." She took his arm and tried to pull him through the door. "I think we need to get those kittens out before they either smother or claw you to death."

Russ resisted her. "I doubt your husband would appreciate it, me bargin' in on Christmas Eve. But if you could call your neighbor, I'd be much obliged."

So news of her marriage had found its way to Russ, after all. "My husband's not here right now. Come in while we sort this out."

He finally stepped over the threshold, although he looked ill at ease. "I had to put them inside my jacket. Steve had this little carrier for them, with red bows and all, but I thought it was way too cold in there. Then when I got here, the little rascals wouldn't go back in that cold little cage. Can't say as I blame 'em."

Jo closed the door behind him and reached for the zipper on his jacket. God, he smelled wonderfully male. "Here." The minute she pulled the zipper partway down, a fuzzy little head poked out, and the first kitten, a tortoiseshell, scrambled free. Jo caught her in one hand and cupped her other hand under the kitten's bottom. "Oh, you little darling! Lucile will love you."

Russ reached inside his jacket and pulled out the second kitten, a tiger-striped gray. "This one's my favorite. No tail." He held the mewing kitten backside out for Jo's inspection.

"For heaven's sake. Must be a manx cat somewhere in her family tree."

"Yep." He cradled the kitten against his chest. "Hush, now, tiger. I'm not hurtin' you none."

No matter how she struggled against it, Jo couldn't help thinking of the last time Russ had stood in her living room, and the magic touch she'd received from the hands that now cuddled a tiny kitten. Desire rushed through her, hot and strong. Very unseemly for a married woman.

To hide her reaction, she inspected the little tortoiseshell. "This one sure looks healthy. Do you know if they've had their shots?"

"Steve took care of that."

"Good. That will help Lucile with the expense, considering there's two."

"That's what Steve figured." Russ's gaze traveled from her Santa hat to her little white boots. The flash of interest in his eyes was brief but unmistakable. "You musta just got home from the Roundup."

Her body responded to that tiny spark. She'd been right about how susceptible she was to him, even though they'd only spent one night in each other's company. It had been, after all, a memorable night. "We closed up early because of the snow."

He surveyed the room, which she'd decorated with a few pine boughs and pinecones along with some sprigs of holly. "Looks nice in here. Smells good, too, with the real tree and all."

"That's the only kind to have." She kept talking to stave off her erotic thoughts. "I decided to get a tree, even if it would only be me enjoying it."

He looked at her in surprise. "What do you mean, only you? Isn't your husband coming home for Christmas?"

In the excitement of having Russ appear on her doorstep she'd forgotten about the story she'd made up for his benefit. "Uh, no, he won't. He had to work."

"On Christmas? Steve said he was some kind of traveling salesman. Surely people wouldn't want to see a salesman on Christmas."

Jo thought fast. "He also services what he sells, and so they needed him for that."

"What needs servicing on Christmas?"

She scrambled through her meager knowledge of essential equipment. "Iron lungs."

"Iron lungs." He stared at her.

Judging from his expression, her tall tale needed some propping up. "I mean, just think of it. It's Christmas Eve and the iron lung malfunctions. Who're you gonna call?"

"Your husband, I reckon."

"You've got it."

Russ stroked the kitten with one hand and it began to purr. "When's he showing up to celebrate Christmas with you, then?"

"Oh, I don't think he'll be able to make it until later in the week." Jo's hunger grew as Russ continued to fondle the little animal. She had total recall of what that fondling was like. "And how can I complain? He's doing such an essential job."

"What's the point in having a salesman for those things? I mean, you either need 'em or you don't. Can't imagine standing around debating the subject."

Jo began to suspect he wasn't going to buy her explanation, but she'd dug this hole and she might as well dig it a little deeper. "Well, there's more than one company that makes them, you see. There's competition, like with everything."

"What's his company?"

"Breath of Life, Inc."

Russ nodded, his gaze speculative. "I have to say, I was kinda surprised to hear you got married."

She forced a laugh. "It was sudden. But I've known—" *Richard? Ronald?* "—that crazy guy for years, and when he showed up and popped the question, we just flew to Vegas and that was that."

"He wasn't the one you were tryin' to forget, was he?"

God, he'd really remembered the details of their encounter. She'd have to be very careful. "No, somebody from before that."

"Somebody you've loved for years, huh?"

She hadn't had this kind of third degree from anybody, and now it had to come from the one person she had to fool. "Well, you know how sometimes you can love somebody, and not really know you love them until something happens. Then all of a sudden, bam! You realize that person is the one for you."

"I can't say I know about that." His gaze pierced hers. "After all, I'm just an Arizona boy."

She'd forgotten about that little zinger she'd asked Steve to leave him with. Apparently it had had some effect. "I suppose you're wondering how I could be so...*free* with you that night and go off and marry somebody else not long afterward."

"It crossed my mind, but then, bein' just an Arizona boy, I must not have made much of an impression on you."

"You were...very nice." What an expert liar she was becoming. Nice didn't even come close. "You turned out to be my last fling—one wild time before I settled down."

He scratched behind the kitten's ears. "And here I was worried about you bein' all upset because I ran out on you, when all I did was clear the way for somebody else."

She looked into his eyes. "You were worried about me being upset?"

"Some."

"Then why didn't you leave me any kind of message?"

He hesitated. "The truth is, I didn't know what to say.

I just—well, I guess it doesn't matter now what I was thinkin' or not thinkin'. Steve told me you'd found somebody, and I'm happy for you."

It mattered a great deal to her what he'd been thinking when he'd walked out of her house that night. Still, she couldn't act too interested in that or she'd give herself away. Maybe it was time to change the subject. "And now you're here delivering everything for Steve and Claire tonight."

"That's right."

"Won't that be kind of difficult, getting it done all by yourself?"

"This is my first stop, so I'm not sure what it'll be like from here on. Steve made out a whole list of instructions, but after dropping it in a snowbank, I can't make out the writing. I let loose of it when one of the kittens scratched me real deep. And then your neighbor wouldn't open her door when I told her I was Santa Claus come to visit."

In spite of the tension of the moment, Jo laughed. "That's what you said?"

"That's what Steve and Claire always say, so I thought I might as well give it a try. Your neighbor left the chain on and hollered through the crack. Told me I was lookin' for love in all the wrong places and to go find somebody my own age to pester."

Jo smiled as she pictured Lucile dealing with this tall cowboy who claimed to be Santa Claus. "I imagine the line worked better for Steve and Claire, because they appeared as a couple and most folks in Prescott know who they are."

"Guess so. Anyway, if you'd call her and tell her I don't mean her any harm, then I can get along with this job."

"Better yet, I'll just walk over there with you." A daring plan had occurred to her. It would be dangerous, but as long as Russ believed she was married, she was confident it would turn out all right. It would mean she wouldn't have to spend Christmas Eve alone, after all, and she might unravel some of the mysteries about this gorgeous cowboy. "In fact, if you like, I could go along when you make the other deliveries."

"You could?" He looked like a drowning man who'd just been thrown a line. "Aw, I couldn't ask you to do that. It's cold out there."

"I'm sure Steve's truck has a heater, and I have warm clothes." She glanced down at her outfit. "I wouldn't go dressed like this, obviously."

"Good."

She glanced up in time to see lust reflected in his eyes and her heart somersaulted with delight. She was playing with fire, but she'd be careful.

He looked away and cleared his throat. "The thing is, I'm not driving Steve's truck. I don't have a license."

"Then how did you get here? In a miniature sleigh with eight tiny reindeer?"

"Sort of." He returned his attention to her. "But the sleigh's full-size, and ol' Blackie has to do the work of the reindeer. He doesn't fly too good, so we've been usin' the roads."

That was when she knew she had to go. She might never have another chance to deliver surprise Christmas presents in a horse-drawn sleigh on Christmas Eve with a Santa who looked like Russ.

She transferred her kitten to him. "Hold them both for a minute and I'll change clothes." She started for the bedroom.

"Wait a minute, Jo."

She turned back to him. "What?"

"Listen, I think I'd best do this alone. I mean, it's my crazy family that started this tradition, so there's no reason to drag somebody else into—"

"Russ, folks expect a man and a woman to be delivering these gifts, and they'll be confused if you show up alone. I'll make the whole thing look more legitimate, and you know it."

"I'll just tell them about Steve and Claire right off instead of using that Santa Claus line."

"Russ, please let me come with you. The only darned thing I have planned is to pop *It's a Wonderful Life* into the VCR. I will die of loneliness spending Christmas Eve by myself, and besides, I've always wanted to ride in a sleigh."

Although there was compassion in his gaze, he shook his head. "I still don't think it's a good idea. What if your husband comes home, thinkin' to surprise you, and finds you out ridin' around in a sleigh with some no-account cowhand?"

"Trust me, he won't be home."

He regarded her for a long moment. "Because he's repairing iron lungs."

"That's right. Just wait there a minute. I won't be long." She ducked into the bedroom.

"Jo?"

"Yes?" she called out as she started unbuttoning her top.

"I'd count it a favor if you'd shut that door."

"Okay." Smiling to herself, she went to do as he asked. His words stroked her ego, even if she couldn't allow his hands to stroke her body. It was nice to know she still tempted him.

"Oh, and Jo?"

"What?"

"Leave the Santa hat on. Some of the folks'll probably get a kick out of it."

"Sure thing." She thought about his last request as she dressed in long underwear, sweats and fur-lined boots. She'd been told Russ had no use for this holiday, but a man who wanted her to wear a Santa hat for their gift-giving journey didn't hate Christmas. Before the night was over, she'd find out why he thought he did.

RUSS JUGGLED the two kittens and tried not to think about Jo getting naked on the other side of the bedroom door. One thing was for sure—her worthless husband didn't deserve her.

Iron lungs. Not likely. Jo was in love, so she believed that hogwash, but Russ wasn't fooled for a minute. He'd been around enough to know the line of bull that certain kinds of lowlifes handed their women.

Jo's husband, Richard something-or-other, according to Steve, was playing around with another honey at this very minute. Russ would lay money on it. In the meantime, Jo, the most wildly passionate woman he'd ever met, was spending her Christmas Eve alone and trying to be brave about it by putting up a tree and decorating the apartment up real nice. It was enough to make him sick.

But he wasn't doing one thing about this sorry situation except to take her along on a sleigh ride. Her husband's being a skunk didn't justify Russ seducing a married woman. He'd committed plenty of sins in his twenty-nine years, but adultery hadn't been one of them. Despite his many failings, he liked to think he wouldn't lower himself to rustle another man's wife, not even if the son of a bitch wasn't fit to call himself a man.

He hoped he hadn't bit off more than he could chew, letting Jo come along tonight. True, he could use the help and he hated thinking of her being all alone on Christmas Eve. But every time he was near her, his blood started pumping faster, and a fair share of it traveled straight to his groin. Good thing she was changing out of that sexy little red outfit, because standing in her living room looking at her a moment ago had been like an instant replay of that November night they'd set each other on fire.

She remembered that night, too. He'd seen it in her eyes. The comment she'd made to Steve pricked him again. *Tell him he was passable for an Arizona boy.* He'd love to know if she really meant that, or if it had been hurt pride talking. But he could hardly ask her. Just talking about the subject was liable to get him hot.

This whole situation might get very sticky if he didn't watch himself. With the Christmas season working on her, and missing her man, she might have entertained the idea of inviting him into her bed again. An Arizona boy who was here had to be more tempting than a Montana boy who wasn't.

Not that she'd follow through on the idea, but she'd probably thought about it. After the way they'd made love that night, it was only natural for her to think about doing it all again. Damn, how he wished they could.

Russ shook his head. This idiot she'd married must have the brain of a chicken, leaving a woman like Jo alone night after night. Russ wouldn't trespass, but sooner or later, some guy would try. It was the way of the world that men caught the scent of a lonely and frustrated wife, and a good many couldn't resist that temptation.

Depending on the circumstances, Jo might be worn

down enough that she'd give in, especially if she began to figure out the holes in her husband's story. Russ ground his teeth. It would happen someday, with some cowboy, sure as shootin'. But by God, he wouldn't be that man. He already had enough on his conscience.

6

AFTER PUTTING ON the Santa hat, Jo shoved her arms into her wool coat, checked to make sure her gloves and muffler were stuffed in the pockets and opened her bedroom door.

Russ looked up.

She couldn't help smiling, seeing such a rough, tough cowhand with his hands full of kittens. He cut quite a figure, as her grandmother would say, standing in front of the multicolored lights of her tree, with Clint Black singing in the background. Couldn't get much more of the yuletide spirit than this—a cowboy, a Christmas tree and kittens.

"I'm ready," she said.

"I hope you put on a lot of clothes."

"I did. I have my long underwear on under the sweats." *And if I owned a chastity belt, I'd be wearing that, too.*

For an unguarded moment he stared at her with heat in his gaze, as if he might be imagining her in the form-fitting underwear. He swallowed and glanced away. "Long underwear's a good idea. I have a couple of warm blankets in the sleigh that we—that you can wrap up in."

Blankets. This was sounding cozier by the minute.

But she had no intention of backing out now. "Then I

guess we might as well take these kittens over to Lucile."

"Do you think she might've gone to bed by now?"

"She's still up. I could hear her television through the wall while I was getting dressed."

His eyes darkened again at the reference to her dressing. He let out a breath. "I think we'd best get going, Jo."

"Sure thing." Damned if she didn't enjoy his discomfort a little bit, perhaps because it did a lot to heal the sore spot he'd left in her heart when he'd walked out on her in the middle of the night. She buttoned her coat and put on her muffler as she moved past him to turn off the Christmas lights and the stereo. "Want me to hold one of the kittens inside my coat?"

"That'd be a help." He handed her the tortoiseshell, and their hands touched briefly. He cleared his throat and backed away. "With two of them it's like a rodeo goin' on in there."

"I'll bet. But I think Steve was right to send two." She tucked the little creature under her coat and opened the door. "Lucile will have such fun watching them play."

"Yeah, ol' Steve knows how to do things right." Russ stepped out into the cold.

Jo heard the wistful tone in Russ's voice, the unspoken message that he didn't know how to do things right like his older brother. Another piece of the puzzle. This would be a very informative evening, she thought, locking up and following Russ to Lucile's door.

Before she'd left for work, she'd shoveled a narrow path down her walkway, and Lucile's. A few inches had fallen since then, but the path was still navigable.

Following Russ gave her a chance to admire him from behind. She could feast her eyes on his broad shoulders and admire the rolling walk of a typical long-legged cowboy, but his cute butt was hidden by the sheepskin jacket. She supplied that image from memory—a memory polished by all the times she'd relived that night they'd spent together.

Sure enough, a red sleigh that looked just like Santa's was parked at her curb, with a black draft horse standing patiently in harness blowing steam from his nostrils.

"Beautiful horse," she said, longing to go make friends with the animal but knowing they had kittens to deliver. "And what an unusual shade of black."

"Steve took a liking to that coat of Blackie's, which is why he bought him. He's mostly Clydesdale, but there's a couple of other breeds mixed in. Steve likes the way he looks with the red sleigh. He means to start up a sleigh-ride business next winter."

"I remember something about that project, but I don't see any seats for passengers."

"He's got a couple benches being upholstered that will fit in the back. But now, with no seats it's a perfect Christmas sleigh."

"It sure is," Jo agreed. "Wasn't he hoping to get you to help him with the sleigh-ride business?"

"Yeah, well, Steve's always cooking up things like that for me. We'll have to see how it goes."

Jo decided not to pursue the subject, but she could sure picture Russ bringing in the tourist trade, as Steve had predicted. The combination of Russ's good looks and the sleigh's romantic image would be dynamite. At the moment, the sleigh looked festive filled with packages of various shapes and sizes.

Wedged among them was an aluminum extension ladder.

"Who gets the ladder?" Jo asked.

"Nobody. That's so's I can climb up on Ned and Sharon's roof."

"Excuse me?"

"Ned and Sharon get a little cooler of champagne, orange juice and a red rose. I gotta lower it down the chimney."

"Good grief."

"I told you this was crazy." He glanced over his shoulder. "No telling when we'll get done with everything, either. You can still back out after we give your neighbor her kittens, if you want. I sure wouldn't blame you."

"Are you kidding? I wouldn't miss this for the world."

"Okay, but don't say I didn't warn you. For all I know, we'll end up getting shot at."

"Has that ever happened to Steve and Claire?"

"Well, no, but everybody knows Steve's truck by now. Nobody's *ever* laid eyes on this-here sleigh. They won't know what's going on."

"Maybe they'll see the sleigh and start believing in Santa Claus again."

"I guess we'll find out." He climbed the two steps leading to Lucile's door, but then he stepped to one side. "You'd better ring the bell. She doesn't want anything to do with me."

Jo stepped up beside him and pushed the doorbell.

Unzipping his jacket a little, Russ stuck his hand inside to cradle the kitten. "Well, tiger, here goes nothing." When no one came immediately, he turned to Jo. "She's probably asleep in front of the TV. I think we should—"

"Give her a minute. It takes her a while to get around."

"I say she's asleep. I say we take the kittens back to Steve."

"Don't give up so easy, Russ. There. She's unlocking the door."

The door opened a crack, but the security chain was still on. "Who is it?" Lucile called.

"It's me, Lucile. Jo."

The chain came off and the door opened wide. Lucile, all five feet of her wrapped in a red quilted bathrobe, her gray hair a cap of ringlets, stood staring at them. "Jo? What on earth are you doing out there this time of night? And why are you with this tipsy cowboy?"

Jo grinned. "He's not drunk, Lucile. This is Russ Gibson, Steve's brother. Steve and Claire are sick, so Russ is taking over their job this Christmas Eve."

"So that's what you meant, young man!" Lucile put a hand to her chest. "Here I was accusing you of being sloshed, and you were trying to bring me a Christmas present. How embarrassing."

Russ touched the brim of his hat. "No problem, ma'am."

"Come in this minute!" She stepped aside to let them by. "I swear, I feel like Ed McMahon just showed up at my door! What a darling little hat, Jo. Come in, come in."

Russ allowed Jo to go ahead of him, and he tipped his hat again as he passed by Lucile. Just then, the tiger-striped kitten began to mew.

"What's that?" Lucile asked, her eyes widening as she turned toward him. "Mercy, that sounds like—"

"It's a kitten, ma'am." Russ hauled the little animal out of his coat. "A no-tailed one, see?" He presented the kitten backside out, just as he had to Jo.

"A...kitten?"

"Two kittens," Jo said, extracting the tortoiseshell. Lucile looked as if she'd gone into shock. Jo hoped this hadn't been a horrible mistake. "They're sisters. One of Steve's barn cats had a late litter. And I, that is, *Santa* thought that you might—"

"Two kittens." Lucile's eyes filled with tears. "Two kittens."

Russ sent a panic-stricken look toward Jo. "You don't have to keep 'em, ma'am. I mean, if this is an imposition, we won't leave them."

"That's right." Jo dumped her kitten in Russ's free hand and hurried over to Lucile as tears streamed down the older woman's face. "This was my harebrained idea, and I can see it was a mistake." She wrapped her arms around Lucile and hugged her tight. "You told me nothing could take Pookie's place, but I just naturally had to try this. Steve's annual visit seemed like the perfect thing. I'm sorry. We'll take them back."

"Over my dead body!" Lucile's response was muffled against Jo's wool coat, but the intent was unmistakable.

Jo stepped back in surprise. "You want them?"

"Right this minute!" Lucile swiped at her eyes and held out both hands. "Bring those little babies to me this minute."

Russ hesitated. "They'll snag your bathrobe, ma'am."

"This bathrobe is already snagged all over from Pookie." Lucile sniffed again. "Bless her heart. She wouldn't want me to be alone, especially when darlings like this need a home. Let me hold those little girls."

Now Jo thought she might cry as Russ walked over and tenderly deposited the kittens, one in each of Lucile's arms.

"The little tiger-stripe likes bein' scratched behind her right ear, especially," Russ said, standing close enough to demonstrate. "See? Her motor's runnin', now. And this little tortoiseshell is partial to bein' rubbed under her chin."

Kittens or women, Jo thought. Russ Gibson made it his business to know how they liked to be stroked.

"I will surely keep those suggestions in mind," Lucile said, her voice husky as she gazed at her twin Christmas presents. She glanced up at him. "Are you sure you can part with these two, young man?"

"Oh, uh, sure." He stepped back and cleared his throat. "I mean, these aren't exactly my kittens in the first place. I just—"

"You just fell in love with them, didn't you?" Lucile said, nuzzling each kitten in turn. "Feel free to come and visit them anytime you like."

"Well, now, I don't really need to do that."

"Russ is more the love-'em-and-leave-'em-type." Jo couldn't believe she'd said it out loud, but there was no taking back the words as Lucile and Russ both looked at her. Russ frowned, but Lucile seemed amused.

"I see," Lucile said, smiling. "Well, Russ, you're welcome, is all I'm saying. No strings attached. And I even keep a few beers in the refrigerator for guests. Which reminds me, I've gone and forgotten my manners. Would either of you like something to eat or drink?"

"That's mighty kind of you, ma'am," Russ said, "but you're the first one on the list, and we'd better get going or we'll be at this until dawn. Ol' Blackie doesn't move as fast as a pickup truck."

"You're doing this on horseback?"

"A horse and sleigh," Jo said. "Now, doesn't that sound like fun?"

Lucile's eyes shone. "It sounds wonderful. If I were twenty years younger, I'd beg to go with you." Her attention returned to the kittens, who had snuggled against the red bathrobe and started kneading their paws into the quilted material as they purred. "But of course I wouldn't want to leave these precious creatures, so I guess I wouldn't beg to go, after all." She looked at Jo. "Thank you, sweetie. This is the best Christmas present I've had in quite a long while."

"You're welcome. But it was Russ and Steve who made it happen." She glanced over at Russ, who was looking as pleased as Jo felt. "It's a fantastic tradition they have. I just sort of piggybacked onto it."

Lucile smiled at Russ. "You must be the silent helper. I always heard about Steve and Claire doing this, but I didn't know you got into the act, too."

"I...usually don't do much," Russ said, looking uncomfortable.

"Good-looking and modest, too. I admire that in a man, don't you, Jo?" She lifted her eyebrows and gave Jo a significant look.

"Uh, yeah. Sure." Jo was afraid she might be blushing.

"I'm sure he appreciates your help tonight."

"I do," Russ said.

"Well, with Richard being away and all, I had the evening free."

"Oh, of course." Lucile's expression wasn't very convincing. "Richard would be away right now."

"Repairing iron lungs," Russ said.

"Doing what?" Lucile stared at Russ.

"Oh, I told you about that," Jo said quickly. "He sells the iron lungs, and then he's on call during holidays, in case an emergency comes up. He can fix small problems himself, you see. You remember me explaining that, don't you, Lucile?"

"Why, uh, yes, I believe I do, now that you mention it." She glanced from Russ to Jo, and merriment danced in her eyes. "I guess you two had better run along, before I—before I keep you from finishing your rounds. I wouldn't want to be responsible for delaying Prescott's own special Santa Claus."

"Before we go, do you need anything for the kittens?" Jo said. "We could rig up a temporary litter box if you need one, and I have some tuna if you—"

"I saved it all," Lucile said gently. "I couldn't bear to get rid of anything to do with Pookie, so I even have a few cans of cat food left, and some toys." She swallowed. "I know Pookie would want me to use them for these little darlings."

"I'm sure she would. She was a loving cat. Merry Christmas, my good neighbor." Her eyes misty, Jo gave Lucile one last hug and each kitten a goodbye caress. Then she headed toward the door.

Russ tipped his hat before starting after Jo. "Merry Christmas, ma'am."

"Call me Lucile, Russ. All of Jo's friends do."

"Merry Christmas, Lucile. Oh, I nearly forgot." Russ pulled a sealed envelope out of the pocket of his coat and handed it to her. "This goes with the kittens. I guess it's a Christmas card."

"How nice." Lucile tucked both kittens in one arm as she stowed the envelope in her bathrobe pocket. "I'll open it later. That way my Christmas surprise will last a little longer. Godspeed, children."

"I'll see you tomorrow," Jo said, waving as she started down the walkway. Her heart was full as she crunched along the snowy sidewalk toward the sleigh. This was what Christmas was all about, and she was very glad she'd asked herself along on this expedition. "I want to go say hello to Blackie," she said.

"Sure, go ahead."

She walked up and held her hand under the horse's muzzle so he could smell her before she began scratching his nose. "Hey, Blackie. Merry Christmas."

Blackie blew out another steamy breath and his eyes drifted half-closed.

"I don't know if I can take too many stops like that," Russ said, coming up to stand beside her.

Jo glanced over at him as she continued to pet Blackie. "Too emotional for you, cowboy?"

"I didn't think she'd start cryin'."

"But they were happy tears. Once I understood that, I was so glad we'd brought her those kittens. We took a chance, though. I guess it could have gone the other way."

Russ stroked Blackie's neck. "I didn't really figure on folks gettin' upset about the presents."

"Maybe *upset* is too strong a word. But the right gift should touch people a little bit, don't you think? Otherwise, what's the point?"

He gazed down at her, the brim of his hat partially shadowing his face. "I don't know," he said, his voice husky. "I haven't had much practice givin' Christmas presents lately."

Lately. That meant something had happened in the recent past to change his approach to the holiday. But despite their intimate night together and her earlier resolve to find out everything about him, she didn't know him well enough to ask about it. "That's too bad. I think you're missing something pretty special."

"That's because you're like most folks, thinkin' there's magic in Christmas."

"Of course I do." She paused and took a deep breath. "But you don't think that."

"Nope."

"Well, that's a shame. But whatever you believe or don't believe, we have a job to do, and we'd better get on with it."

"You're right about that. And I'm powerful glad you're going with me, Jo. I'll let you handle the waterworks, if we get any more."

"We'll see," she said, deliberately leaving her response vague. She wasn't about to shield him from emotions he might encounter tonight. He'd never understand about magic if he didn't allow himself to feel.

Russ gave Blackie a pat. "I guess we'd better get going."

"I guess so. You're doing great, Blackie." With one final rub down his nose, she walked back to the sleigh where Russ stood waiting.

"Up you go." He steadied her as she climbed onto the driver's bench at the front of the sleigh.

She reacted to that firm grip as she had the other times they'd made physical contact, from the first moment in his arms when they began dancing at the Roundup. Her knees grew weak and without him holding her upright, she made a clumsy job of getting into the sleigh.

He had to grab her around the waist to prevent her from tumbling sideways.

"Sorry," she said. "I'm not used to getting into these, I guess."

"You probably just slipped on the step. It's slippery from the snow."

"Yeah, that's probably it." Her breathing unsteady, she picked up the soft blanket that was folded on the seat and sat down with it on her lap.

"Just a second. Almost forgot Blackie's treat." Russ walked to the horse and pulled a plastic bag from his jacket pocket. "Hey, boy, did you think I forgot about this, huh?" he crooned, taking a piece of carrot out of the bag. "I wouldn't do that, Blackie. Just got distracted. I won't let it happen again." He cupped his hand beneath the horse's muzzle and scratched along the crest of his mane as Blackie chomped the carrot.

Jo gazed at Russ, adding more pieces to the puzzle. He didn't give Christmas presents, but he'd filled his pockets with bits of carrot to reward his horse during the night's journey. He kept trying to pretend he didn't go in for sloppy emotions, but his actions made a liar out of him.

With a final scratch behind the ears for Blackie, Russ returned to the sleigh and swung up beside Jo. There wasn't a lot of room between them, and his arm brushed against her as he pulled on gloves and leaned forward to gather up the reins. "Wrap that blanket around you," he said. "You'll need it."

"But you won't?"

"Nah. I'm used to it. Claire made me bring that blanket, and there's a couple more in back." He clucked to Blackie and slapped the reins against the horse's rump. The sleigh lurched and then began gliding over the snowpacked street with a soft hissing sound. Blackie's hooves crunched rhythmically as he trotted along and the bells on his harness jingled.

The cold wind created by their movement caught Jo by surprise, and she quickly unfolded the blanket.

"Told you." Russ grinned at her.

"I'm f-fine." Jo wrapped the blanket around her knees and pulled it up to her armpits. It was a soft plush in bright red and more sensuous than Jo would have expected to find in a rancher's sleigh. No doubt Steve had bought it with an eye toward pleasing the tourists he'd be taking on rides one day soon.

"You're not fine. Your teeth are chattering," Russ said. "I can still take you back home."

"Nope. I'm g-going. What's next?"

"Ned and Sharon's."

"The ladder."

"Yep. I have that one figured out, but once we get past Ned's, I'll need help figuring out the list."

"See, you need m-me." She blinked as the frigid wind brought moisture to her eyes.

He gave her a long glance. Then he sighed. "Come here, woman," he said, wrapping his arm around her and pulling her close, "before you freeze to death."

7

HOLDING JO CLOSE felt way too good, Russ thought. But he didn't know what else to do. She'd been shivering real bad, and the wind was making her eyes water. He couldn't very well leave her like that and have her catch a cold or something because he was scared of putting his arm around her and keeping her warm.

Maybe he could pretend she was Claire. He'd hugged Claire plenty of times, or rather she'd hugged him and he'd squeezed back, so's not to appear unfriendly. Claire was the type to start the hugging business with folks she liked, and for some reason, she liked him. Putting his arms around Claire felt comforting, to be honest, so he didn't mind her hugging him a lot.

Putting his arm around Jo didn't feel comforting at all. He'd hoped with those layers she'd put on, he wouldn't feel her heat through the padding. But he could feel it, and it called to him on a level his mind couldn't control. The scents he linked with her—the shampoo she used on her hair, her classy perfume, and underneath those artificial things the special fragrance of Jo—all combined to turn his brain to mush. For weeks he'd tried to push her out of his mind, but now he realized she'd taken up permanent space there. He wanted her more than ever.

Just having her nestled against him like this was enough to start him thinking about ways to have her, and he'd even congratulated himself on having a condom available in his wallet. But she was *married*, dammit. Untouchable, according to his personal code. She'd cuddled in real easy, too, fitting right inside the crook of his arm as if made to go there.

Maybe it was the lack of sex that was bothering him. He'd been so obsessed with Jo ever since that November night that he'd been totally uninterested in anybody else. Logic told him that the best cure for one woman was to take a different one to bed, but he hadn't been able to make himself do it. So now here he was, in dangerous contact with the woman he wanted, who just happened to be the woman he couldn't have. Damnation.

"Russ?"

He shifted on the seat slightly to ease the ache in his groin. "What?"

"Ned told me that Sharon was planning a real intimate evening for the two of them, if you know what I mean."

"I reckon I do."

"So wouldn't that include a fire in the fireplace? How're you going to lower a cooler down a chimney if there's a fire going?"

Just her talking to him while she was so close was driving him crazy. It reminded him of the way they'd talked to each other while they'd made love. He didn't remember another woman ever telling him he'd caused her bones to melt, or that she felt nailed to the bed. Oh, Lord, but he wanted to do those things again.

"Stumped you, huh?" she said.

He'd totally lost track of her question. "About what?"

"The fireplace. I think they'll have a fire in it. And a bearskin rug in front of it."

"You sound experienced in such goings-on."

"A little bit."

Yeah, he'd just bet. He could easily picture Jo stretched out naked on a bearskin rug. He shifted on the seat again, although no amount of moving around would take care of his problem.

"Are you saddle sore, Russ? You keep twitching around."

"Something like that."

"Maybe you should have brought a pillow."

And her four-poster to go with it, he thought. "I'll be okay."

"If you say so. So what about the fireplace?"

"Steve figured they'd be in—" He paused to clear his throat. This was not a good subject to be discussing with Jo. "He figured they'd be in bed by now, so the champagne and orange juice would be for Christmas mornin'. If there's smoke comin' out of the chimney, we'll leave the cooler by the front door, ring the bell and take off. I know Steve wanted this to be a hit-and-run situation so's not to disturb...whatever they're doin'."

"I don't picture a fast getaway in this rig."

"Don't worry. It'll be fast enough." He turned down the quiet little street where Ned lived. Christmas lights sparkled along the eaves of many of the houses, pine wreaths hung on the doors and snowmen stood grinning at them from a couple of front yards. Russ pulled up in front of Ned's house with some relief. He needed to be doing something besides holding on to this tempting woman beside him and talking about people on bearskin rugs and such.

"Here we are, and I don't see smoke," he said. "All the lights are out, too." He could just imagine what those newlyweds were up to. In his present condition, it didn't bear thinking about. Ned and Sharon wouldn't hear a stampede on their roof, let alone one cowboy with a Christmas cooler.

"No lights." Jo moved from the protection of his arm and peeled away the blanket. "Maybe Sharon went for the bubble-bath-and-candlelight seduction instead."

Russ clenched his jaw. "Could we maybe talk about something else besides Ned and Sharon's goings-on?"

She gazed at him, and except for the gleam in her eye, her expression was innocent enough. "You seem kinda touchy for a swingin' bachelor. Haven't the women in Tucson been treating you right?"

"I'd as soon not talk about my sex life, either."

"Hey, don't be shy. After all, we've had some good times, you and I. You can tell Jo your troubles."

"Thanks, but you don't look like no Dear Abby to me." He looped the reins through the brass handrail. "Time for me to play Santa Claus and climb up on ol' Ned's roof." He got down from the sleigh. "You can stay wrapped up here in the blanket, if you want."

"No, I'll help. That's what I'm supposed to be here for."

He'd begun to wonder if she was here to torment him with the fact that he couldn't have her. He hadn't thought of revenge as a motive when she'd made her offer to accompany him. "Then if you don't mind, I could use somebody to steady the ladder." Truth to tell, he wasn't crazy about heights, although he'd never made much of a fuss about it. Steve didn't know how queasy he got once he was more than ten feet off the ground. When he was a kid, he'd been afraid Steve and his friends would make fun of him for it. Now that he was grown, he felt foolish admitting to such a thing.

"I'd be glad to hold the ladder." She scooted over and started to climb down.

He remembered she'd had trouble getting up, and he automatically helped her down. Big mistake. Once he had his hands around her waist, he couldn't seem to let go again. He set her on her feet and just stood there, close enough to kiss her, his hands still spanning her waist.

She didn't seem inclined to move, either. She gazed up at him, her hands resting lightly on his shoulders, her mouth full and inviting.

"You shouldn't look at a man that way that unless you intend to kiss him." His voice was low with frustration.

"I do feel like kissing you." Her breath made puffy little clouds in the still air.

It was a strange sensation, iciness on his face, a furnace burning in his groin. "Have you forgotten about that little gold band on your finger, lady?"

"When I'm with you, it's hard to remember."

He was having trouble remembering, himself. She felt so right in his arms. "Jo, tell me the truth. Are you thinkin' about cheating on your husband?"

"What would you say if I was?"

"I've got no right to judge anybody. I'd say you have to do what you have to do. It just ain't gonna be with me."

"Are you so sure about that?" She settled in against him and lifted her face to his.

He fought back his natural instincts to tighten his grip and claim what she was offering. "Now listen here, sweetheart. If you hadn't gone and got yourself hitched, I'd love you six ways to Sunday right this minute, long underwear notwithstandin'."

Her eyes grew round. "Right here? How?"

"The bed of the sleigh would work out just fine, honey, and I'm sure I could find my way through all the clothes you have on, considering the reward I'd get for it. But I don't make love to married women. I don't have many rules for myself, but that's one I don't intend to break, even for somebody as temptin' as you are. If your new husband doesn't do you right, if he's leavin' you alone and unsatisfied, get rid of him. Then come and see me. Until then, you're off limits." Feeling noble as hell, he released her and stepped back.

The look on her face just about killed him. Judging from her behavior, the bastard she'd married wasn't giving her any satisfaction, because she needed loving more than any woman he'd ever seen. He hated watching misery, in people or animals, but Jo had chosen her path and she'd need to work her way out of her mistake without him adding to her confusion.

"I'll get the ladder," he said, heading toward the back of the sleigh.

WELL, now she'd done it, Jo thought. Her bruised ego had demanded to know that Russ still wanted her, so she'd been testing him, taunting him a little to make up for the way he'd deserted her that November night. She'd expected him to put the moves on her eventually, and then she'd have her little moment of revenge when she regretfully turned him down because she was married.

To her surprise, she'd uncovered a bedrock of moral strength in Russ that she'd never suspected was there, given his reputation. He'd been the one to do the rejecting, leaving her filled with frustration and a grudging admiration. Lots of men might pretend not to notice a married woman when folks were watching, like at the Roundup. But Jo didn't know many who would deny themselves if that same woman offered sexual favors in private, as Jo had just done.

She already knew Russ was an exceptional lover. She hadn't expected to learn that he had all these admirable scruples, too. Yet none of what she knew squared with his behavior when he'd left her in the middle of the night. No matter how self-sacrificing he seemed at the moment, she couldn't forget that he was also capable of being completely insensitive.

To make matters worse, the picture he'd painted of finding a way through the layers of clothes she'd put on, of making love in the sleigh because he was too aroused to wait for a more convenient spot, really turned her on. She wondered if she could erase that picture from her mind, or if it would tempt her for the rest of the night.

He'd started across the yard with the ladder under his arm and the cooler and rope clutched in his free hand. She had, after all, said she'd help him with this job. She hurried after him, floundering a little in the deep snow.

He stopped and turned. "Be careful, now, Jo. Don't go hurtin' yourself."

"I'm fine." She panted a little from the effort of tramping through the drifts.

He glanced at her path and smiled. "If you'd follow where I've been walkin', it would go easier."

"Maybe I'm having fun doing it this way." On impulse she held out both arms and fell straight backward.

"What in tarnation?" He dropped both the ladder and the cooler and plowed through the snow to where she'd fallen. "Did you faint or somethin'?" He sank to one knee beside her.

She gazed up at him as she swished her arms and legs through the snow. "Nope. I'm making a snow angel.

Christmas Eve seems like the perfect time for one, don't you think?''

The concern in his eyes gave way to exasperation.

"You scared the wits out of me, woman."

"Sorry."

His expression softened.

"I'd plum forgot about snow angels."

"Russ, could we...pretend that we didn't have that conversation out by the sleigh? I don't want you to think I'm some sort of loose woman."

"Don't go blamin' yourself. From the look of things, he's not giving you the good loving you should have every blessed night of your life."

Oh, God, but she'd put herself in a pickle. She could scarcely breathe from wanting him. "But you certainly did give me good loving, Russ."

He smiled. "For an Arizona boy."

"I just said that because I was mad at you. You were very good to me, Russ."

"Couldn't help myself. You were made for loving, little darlin'."

The fierce ache within her grew stronger. "I really need to know why you left without a word that night."

His gaze darkened and he started to say something. Then he looked away.

"Why?" she persisted.

When he looked back at her, his expression had closed down. "Doesn't matter now."

"Maybe it does."

"I can't see why. You and me aren't involved anymore." He held out his hand. "Let me help you up so you don't smear your angel. And then we got things to do."

She allowed him to pull her carefully out of the snow.

"I'd count it a special favor if you'd explain about that night."

He rested his hands on her shoulders. "I'm not gonna tell you, Jo. Especially not tonight. And if you pester me about it, I swear to God I'll turn ol' Blackie around and take you home again. It'll make me a little late deliverin' the Christmas presents, but I'll manage."

She studied him for a long moment. "Okay, I won't pester you. Subject's closed. Let's get that ladder set up."

As they worked to expand the ladder and lean it against the house without making too much noise, Jo thought about her choices. She wouldn't get the full story out of Russ unless she told him that her marriage was a fake. Even then he might be so furious at being tricked that he wouldn't explain himself. But it was her only chance to find out what had been going on in his mind when he'd decided to walk out of her house.

Of course, if she told him her marriage wasn't real, then she'd leave the way open for him to "love her six ways to Sunday," as he'd so colorfully put it, in the bed of the sleigh this Christmas Eve. Just the thought made her hotter than a pizza oven. But she'd also be leaving herself open to more heartbreak, and risking her education plans if she became obsessed with this cowboy and he walked out on her again. She'd better not make any quick decision about tearing down the defense she'd so carefully built up.

Russ put his foot on the first rung of the ladder and picked up the cooler. "I hope ol' Ned appreciates this," he said.

"I'm sure he will. Sharon will, too."

Russ climbed up a few rungs and looked down. "Have you got a good hold on that ladder?"

"I'm holding on real tight."

"You might want to brace yourself across it, so it doesn't slide on the snow."

"Okay." Jo followed his instructions.

He climbed a little higher before glancing down again. "Don't let go, okay?" he called softly.

"I won't let go." She watched him slowly mount another few rungs. He looked very tentative, very unlike the bold cowboy she knew. "Russ, are you afraid of heights?"

"Who, me?"

So he was. She smiled to herself. "Come on down. I'll take the cooler up there. I've never minded high places."

"Nope." He continued to make his painfully slow way up the ladder. "I promised Steve, and I ain't letting you take the job and maybe have something happen to you."

"Does Steve know you're afraid of heights?"

"Not exactly. And I'm not *afraid*. Just real cautious."

"I see." She tried to keep the amusement from her voice. "Well, I'm an expert at holding a ladder, so you'll be safe with me. I used to hold the ladder for my daddy all the time back in Montana. He never fell once."

"That's a comfort." Eventually he reached the roofline of the two-story house. His voice drifted down to her. "There's a lot of snow up here."

"Crawl on your hands and knees, and take it easy," Jo said, staring up at him.

"On my hands and knees? I can't do that. It's not dignified."

"It's a lot more dignified than sliding off the roof and flipping headfirst into a snowbank."

"I wish you hadn't said that."

"Stay on your hands and knees and it won't happen."

"What if somebody sees me crawling around like some sissy up here?"

"I'll just tell them you lost your contacts."

He laughed softly. "Yeah, you do that." He hefted the cooler to the roof and crawled tentatively after it. On his hands and knees, as Jo had suggested, he moved away from the edge and toward the chimney that rose from the middle of the roof.

Jo soon lost sight of him and could only keep track of where he was by the steady scraping sound as he inched across the roof. She leaned against the ladder and chalked up one more endearing trait for this cowboy. He was afraid of heights, but he wouldn't let that stop him from doing the job his brother had asked of him. That demonstrated more courage, as far as Jo was concerned, than getting on the back of a Brahma bull.

How peaceful it was on this Christmas Eve, she thought, gazing up at the stars that glittered in a sky swept clear of clouds. She could almost imagine that Santa Claus himself was up there, guiding his team of reindeer through the night. Maybe traveling around with Russ and delivering presents made such fantasies seem possible. There was magic in Christmas, and with luck she'd be able to convince Russ that it was so.

Her blissful trance ended as blinding light flooded the house and yard. "Freeze," barked an amplified male voice. "You by the ladder, hands on your head. You on the roof, come down the ladder nice and easy. Your little party's over, folks."

With a groan, Jo folded her hands on top of her Santa hat and shut her eyes in dismay. So much for peace on earth. The cops had arrived. "We're not robbers, Officer!" she called. "We're delivering Christmas presents!"

"Oh, is that it? And I suppose those packages in the

sleigh are what you're giving away, instead of the stuff you've taken so far."

"That's right. And I need to hold the ladder for Russ, so that—"

"Your partner can make it down just fine, ma'am. Keep those hands on your head."

Jo gazed upward as Russ started to back down the ladder. It wobbled and she held her breath. For someone afraid of heights, coming down was probably harder than going up.

Just as Russ drew level with the second story, the window right beside him shot up with a bang.

"What in hell's goin' on?" Ned bellowed into the night.

Russ jerked backward and the ladder began to fall.

"Jump into the bushes!" Jo yelled.

Russ let go of the ladder and launched himself at some snow-covered evergreen bushes next to the house. His pushoff sent the ladder clanging to the ground on Jo's left, while Russ flew through the air on her right. His hat plopped down at her feet just before he landed in a cloud of snow and snapping branches.

"Russ!" No longer caring what the police had in mind for her, Jo ran over to where he lay facedown, not moving.

8

AFTER YEARS of getting bucked off horses and bulls, Russ knew better than to move quickly and risk hurting himself worse, especially considering there was no animal bearing down on him at the moment. The breath was knocked clean out of him, and snow was jammed into his eyes, his mouth and up his nose, but he managed to painfully draw a little air into his lungs. He flexed his fingers and toes. So far, so good.

"Oh, Russ, please don't be dead!"

That would be Jo talking, he thought. She sounded really worried about him, as if she cared what happened to his sorry carcass. That felt kinda nice.

"Russ?" She touched his hair. "Russ?" There was a choking sound, as if she might be starting to cry.

His chest still felt as if somebody had cinched a saddle around him good and tight, but he didn't want her to cry. "I'm...okay," he said, gasping.

"We'll take care of him," said some guy, probably one of the cops.

Jo stopped stroking his head and there was a metal click, like handcuffs snapped together. They weren't fastened on him, so it had to be Jo they'd handcuffed. That would never do.

"Hey!" Jo cried. "What's that for?"

"You're under arrest."

As Russ listened to the officer reading Jo her rights, he

knew he had to get up and take care of this disaster, but trying to get out of the snowy bush was like climbing off a giant marshmallow. Finally, he just rolled off and ended up on his butt staring at the two officers and Jo, whose hands were behind her back. He didn't recognize either of the cops, which would make this explanation tougher.

The one with Jo was short and on the pudgy side. The one hovering over him was taller, younger and meaner-looking. Must be new guys—new guys would probably draw duty on Christmas Eve while the veterans got to stay home with their families.

Russ focused on the pudgy one. "Take the cuffs off that woman."

"Sorry, buddy, can't do it."

"We've even got a matching pair for you," said the tall guy next to Russ. In no time he'd cuffed Russ's hands behind his back and was reading him his rights, too.

Peachy. "Look, Officer, my name is Russ Gibson. My brother's Steve Gibson, who owns the Double G Ranch. We were just—"

"Then let's see some ID."

"Uh, I don't have any."

"How convenient."

"Hey, guys!" Ned called from the open window. "Could somebody fill me in on what's happenin' down there?"

"Looks like Bonnie and Clyde here were cooking up some holiday plans of their own," one of the cops said.

"Wrong." Russ glanced toward the second story. "It's me, Ned. Steve and Claire took sick, so I'm playin' Santa this year. Jo's helping me."

Ned stared out the window. "Russ? I didn't even know you was in town."

"Just got in this mornin'."

"And Steve's got you passing out presents? I don't believe it."

One of the officers pulled Russ to his feet. "Seems he doesn't believe your little story. He'll be wanting to press charges, I imagine." He picked up Russ's hat from the ground and slapped it on his head. "Let's go, cowboy."

"Hey! Take me if you have to, but let her go. And somebody's got to see to my horse. I—"

"Wait!" Ned called. "I believe he's playing Santy Claus! I was just surprised for a minute. Ain't you guys heard about Steve and Claire Gibson's Christmas Eve rounds? They've been doin' it for years."

The officer guiding Jo to the patrol car turned to the window. "Yeah, and we were given a description of his truck so we'd recognize it." He gestured toward the horse and sleigh. "That's not it."

Ned craned his neck to see out into the street in front of the house. "I'll be horn-swoggled, Russ. Damned if you didn't bring the sleigh. Hey, Officers! That's Steve Gibson's sleigh. He's been restoring it so's he can give rides one of these days. This ol' boy had to use it because he don't have no driver's license. You all wait there 'til I get my pants on. I'm comin' down."

Both officers paused. The tall one shrugged as he looked at the pudgy one. "I guess we might as well wait, Hank."

Russ glanced at Jo. "Are you okay?"

"I'm okay. How about you?"

"I'll be better if we don't spend Christmas in the pokey."

"We won't. Ned won't let that happen."

Russ grimaced. "I guess we interrupted his special evening, after all."

"Don't worry about it." She smiled at him. "It'll make a good story to tell his grandchildren."

"Here I come," Ned called from the porch. He started across the snowy yard. "Now just take the cuffs off those folks, you hear? They didn't mean no harm."

The tall cop with Russ hesitated. "You're willing to vouch for them, then?"

"Hell, yes." Ned finished zipping his sheepskin coat and turned up the collar as he reached them. "I know ol' Russ real good, and Jo's new in town, but she's okay, too. Trust me, they're out deliverin' Christmas gifts, just like they said they was." He looked at Russ and grinned. "What'd you bring me, Santy Claus?"

"It ain't for you, cowboy. It's for Sharon. I lowered it down the chimney."

"And whose bright idea was that?" Ned asked, blowing on his hands.

"I think Claire's."

"Figures. Hey, you fellows gonna take off those cuffs or not? I don't like to see my friends standin' here looking like criminals."

"Guess so," said the tall cop. He unlocked Russ's handcuffs. "We'd better not catch you two doing anything else suspicious tonight."

"We've got more deliveries to make." Russ rubbed his wrists and walked over to put a protective arm around Jo. "I don't want to be running into you guys every five minutes."

"Any more presents going down the chimney?" asked the pudgy cop.

"Nope. For the rest we'll either knock on the door or just leave them on the porch."

"Then we won't have any more trouble," said the tall cop.

"Merry Christmas," added the pudgy one as the officers got into the patrol car. Then they drove away, the car's snow tires crunching on the hard-packed surface.

Ned looked at Russ and started to chuckle. "That was some swan dive, pardner. You okay?"

"I've been hurt worse fallin' off a bar stool," Russ said.

"You two want to come in for a cup of coffee or somethin'?"

"Thanks, but I think we'd better get going," Jo said.

"Besides," Russ said, "I think we've done enough damage to your evenin'." He paused. "I, uh, don't suppose you'd keep this little matter to yourself, would you?"

Ned laughed. "I don't know. What's it worth to you?"

"How about if I promise never to tell Sharon about that night we spent drinkin' beer in the stock tank?"

"I could live without her knowin' about that."

"I'd appreciate it, Ned. Honest to God, if Steve finds out we nearly got arrested—"

"Correction. You did get arrested. I got you unarrested."

"True."

"Ned, honey?" called a sweet voice from the front door. "Are you coming back to bed?"

"Go back to your bride," Russ said, clapping Ned on the shoulder. "And a merry Christmas to the both of you."

"Same here," Jo said.

"Thanks. You, too." Ned started across the yard and

turned back, scratching his head. "You know, Russ, that might be the first time you ever wished me a merry Christmas."

"I always wished you a merry Christmas, Ned. I just didn't say so."

Ned smiled. "It works a whole lot better when you say it. Good night now."

Jo and Russ each called good-night and started toward the sleigh.

"If you want me to take you home, I wouldn't blame you," Russ said. He removed his hat and turned the brim in his hand, repairing the damage from the fall. The hat was damp, but basically okay. "I'm sure you didn't figure on bein' handcuffed during the evenin'."

"Are you kidding? I wouldn't dream of leaving now. This will also give me something to tell my grandchildren."

A horrible thought occurred to him, stopping him dead in his tracks. "Hold on, Jo."

"What?"

"Please don't tell me you're carryin' that fellow's baby."

She looked startled. "No, I'm not. But where did that come from?"

He let out his breath in a whoosh of relief. "The way you started talkin' about your grandchildren, I thought maybe the process was already started. Though I can't imagine how he'd have accomplished it, as little as he's—"

"Well, I'm not pregnant."

"Good. Because once a baby comes along, it's hard to split the sheets. I'd be careful if I was you."

They reached the sleigh and she turned to him. "You're really worried about me, aren't you?"

"Naturally. You're a sweet-lovin' woman, and I'd like to see you settled real nice." He couldn't admit how her marriage had affected him, as if a mule had kicked him in the gut.

Even though he had nothing to offer and wouldn't have dreamed of asking her to marry him, it drove him crazy to think of her married to someone else. Now that he knew the guy was a low-down skunk, he was determined to see them separated. If they did split, he still ought to stay the hell away from her, so it was more for her sake than his that he wanted the breakup. At least that's what he kept telling himself.

"I'm touched, Russ. I really am. You have a tender heart. And you know, considering that, I keep wondering how it is that..."

"What?"

"Nothing. I promised I wouldn't pester you."

So they were back to that. And as long as they were, he had to ask one last question of his own. It made him nervous to ask it, and he tapped his hat against his thigh in agitation. "Okay, I need the answer to a question, myself. My leavin' in the middle of the night—did that have anything at all to do with you running off and marryin' that guy so quick?"

She gazed at him, her eyes reflecting the starlight above her, her voice soft as the night. "What do you think?"

He groaned. "Damnation. I was afraid of that."

"It hurt when you left, Russ."

"I know." Damn, he thought. Damn, damn, *damn*. "I'm sorry. I didn't mean to cause you to do something like this. I feel terrible."

"You know what? I wish you'd kiss me," she murmured. "Just once, for old time's sake. Pretend we're under the mistletoe."

He tossed his hat to the seat of the sleigh. Then he gathered her gently into his arms, meaning to give her a kiss of apology.

"I'm truly sorry, Jo," he said quietly, brushing his lips over hers. "So sorry, honey."

She whimpered and pulled him closer.

He hadn't intended it to become that kind of kiss. He tried to keep things civilized, but finally control went out the window as he met the heat and hunger of her mouth. If she'd been sizzling the first night they'd made love, she was a raging fire tonight.

Before he knew it, he'd thrust his tongue deep and started unbuttoning her coat. It took him seconds to reach inside, pull up her sweatshirt and start unsnapping the front of her long underwear. He didn't realize what he was doing until he cupped her bare breast and she moaned and pressed her nipple against his palm.

He pulled his hand out as if he'd touched a stove burner, whirled and braced both arms against the sleigh.

"Button up," he said, breathing hard.

"Russ—"

"I helped get you into this fix, and I feel bad about that. But making love to you now won't set anything right, no matter how much we want each other. I won't step out of line again. But I'm beggin' you, Jo, tell that no-account husband of yours to take a hike. You're not in love with him. Not when you can kiss me like that."

"You're right." She sounded out of breath. "I'm not in love with him."

Are you in love with me? He didn't have the right to ask the question and didn't really want to know the answer. The hell he didn't.

"Who's...who's next on the list?" she asked.

He reached in his jacket pocket, pulled out the water-stained piece of paper and handed it to her without turning around. He wasn't quite ready to face her yet. One look into those big eyes of hers and he might just haul her back into his arms. In a minute he'd be stronger. He had to be.

"The name's—" She paused and cleared her throat. "The name's kind of washed away, but it looks like the next person gets a hand-crocheted baby blanket. Does that mean anything to you?"

"Yep. Elaine Overton."

"I think I know her." Her voice was steadier now. "She took a class at Yavapai, but as I remember, she couldn't finish it because of the baby."

"And there were other reasons, too, accordin' to Claire. I was thinkin' about Elaine when I warned you not to get pregnant." He gazed up at the cold light of the stars. "Her husband left about two months before the baby came, so now raisin' the little one will be up to her."

"That's terrible."

"Claire thought so, too. She crocheted the blanket, figuring something handmade would cheer Elaine up and keep the baby warm all at the same time."

"What a wonderful idea." She touched him on the arm. "Ready to go?"

He took a deep breath. "Yep."

She climbed into the sleigh and he resisted the impulse to help her up. He reached in the back and tossed her another blanket. "Bundle up good. We gotta make time, so I'm giving ol' Blackie his head." After taking some more carrots to the patient horse, he swung up beside Jo. "Time to dash away, dash away all." He slapped the reins on Blackie's rump and soon they were whizzing down the snowy street.

"I didn't think you'd know that poem," Jo said.

"Which one?"

"'Twas the Night Before Christmas.'"

"I know it. And I can sing most all the carols if I've a mind to. I just don't have a mind to."

"Then maybe I will, if that's okay."

"Go right ahead. Blackie, he likes singing."

"How about Russ?"

"He don't mind it, neither."

"Okay. Then I might as well start with 'Jingle Bells.'"

She sang with enthusiasm and she had a real pleasing voice, in Russ's opinion. The song lifted his spirits and brought a smile, in spite of himself.

"How's that?" she asked, turning to him.

"Real nice. Do you know 'What Child Is This?'"

"Of course. It's one of my favorites." She glanced at him. "You're welcome to join in."

"I like listenin' to you." In fact, he couldn't help thinking, as they whipped through the cold, clear night, that it would be a blessing to live in the same house with a woman who enjoyed singing. He wondered if she'd ever done that with her husband around, and if he had the brains to appreciate it.

CHRISTMAS CAROLS had never seemed to hold such meaning as they did tonight, Jo thought. Steve and Claire were onto something, giving out surprise presents all around town. She wondered if Russ would go along next year, now that he realized how much fun it was. Of course, they wouldn't need her, much as she'd love to be in on it again.

Lights were on in the tiny bungalow where Elaine and

her baby lived. A small tree perched on a table in the front window, and a pine-bough wreath, obviously homemade, hung on the door.

Russ stopped the sleigh and hopped down. He offered Jo a hand, but he let go as soon as her feet touched ground, as if to make sure their brief touch didn't become more. Reaching in the back, he pulled out the gaily wrapped package tied with a red bow and a rattle. Even before they reached the door, they could hear the wail of a baby.

"Sounds like Elaine has her hands full tonight," Jo said. "She doesn't have any folks nearby?"

"They're in Texas, and didn't think she shoulda married the guy. Claire says Elaine's too proud to tell them what happened." He rang the doorbell.

"Oh." Jo understood that kind of pride far too well. "Poor woman."

Elaine peeked out the window.

Then she hurried to open the door, the baby squirming and crying against her shoulder. "Goodness, if it isn't Russ Gibson! Come right in. And Jo Cassidy, is that you? Remember me from folklore class?"

"I sure do."

"Merry Christmas, Elaine," Russ said. "We brought you a little something. It's for Amanda, really."

Despite the baby's crying, her expression brightened. "A Christmas gift for us? Oh, you didn't have to do that!" She closed the door and jiggled the baby. "Shush, now, Amanda. We have company. We have—" She smiled at Russ. "We have Santa paying us a visit."

The baby kept crying.

"We're filling in for Steve and Claire," Russ said, unzipping his jacket with one hand as he held the package in the other. "They took sick all of a sudden."

"Did you come in a sleigh?" She eyed the bright package with obvious delight as she rocked the baby back and forth. The wailing continued. "I could have sworn there was a sleigh parked out front, but maybe I was seeing things."

"It's a sleigh," Jo said. "We're having a great time riding around passing out the things Steve and Claire gathered together."

"It sounds wonderful." Elaine's cheer slipped a little. "It sounds—" She began to sniffle. "Oh, dear. Excuse me." She turned away.

Russ looked at Jo, his expression pleading.

She could have gone over to comfort Elaine and the baby, as she had with Lucile. But this was his gig, not hers. She took the package from him and tipped her head toward Elaine.

He took a deep breath and walked over to put his hand on Elaine's trembling shoulder. "Let me take that little one for a minute. You look like you could use a break."

"Oh, no, Russ." Elaine's voice was weak and fluttery. "She's so fussy tonight. I think it's a touch of colic. I couldn't ask—"

"You didn't. I offered." He reached down and gently lifted the crying baby from Elaine's arms. "Hey, there, Amanda. What's your problem, sweetheart? A little tummyache?" He cradled the baby against his shirt and began to amble around the room, talking to her in a low tone.

Gradually the wailing turned to whimpers, then a few hiccups, then blissful silence as Amanda snuggled in, her face against the sheepskin lining of Russ's jacket.

Elaine sagged against a nearby chair. "Goodness.

She's been crying all night, it seems. I don't know how you did that, Russ."

Jo was pretty impressed, herself. If she thought about it, though, his way with babies fit with everything else she was learning about him. Natural kindness and empathy had a way of soothing animals and people alike.

"Maybe it was the sound of a different voice," Russ said. "She had to stop and listen to figure out who this joker was who had ahold of her."

"Whatever it was, I'm so grateful. Would you like a cup of tea or something?"

"Sure," Jo said, glancing at Russ. "I'll help." She figured Elaine needed the tea as much as anyone.

He nodded and kept murmuring to the baby, whose delicate eyelids were drifting closed.

Jo gazed at him for a moment before laying the present under the tree and following Elaine into the kitchen. He probably didn't even like tea, she thought, yet he understood they were needed here for a while longer. He looked so darned sweet holding the baby that tenderness brought a lump to Jo's throat.

"The tea's in the second cupboard," Elaine said, putting the water on to heat. "I have a couple of kinds."

"Amanda's beautiful." Jo took the tea boxes from the cupboard.

"When she's not screaming, she certainly is." Elaine brought down three mugs and arranged several tea bags in a little bowl. "But sometimes I just don't know what to do."

"It must be very hard."

Elaine met her gaze. "I won't kid you. Not having her father around to help isn't easy." She hesitated. "This is probably none of my business, but I thought you were married, too. Did he—"

"Leave?" Jo discovered she had no interest in making up more stories. They'd begun to sound wrong. "In a way."

"Oh, honey, I'm sorry." Elaine gave her a quick hug. "Men can be bastards, can't they?"

"Some of them."

"But those Gibson boys are A-number-one. I don't know Russ very well, but he seems to be every bit as terrific as his brother."

"He's a lot different from Steve, that's for sure."

"And just between us, a lot cuter. Are you two involved?"

"No. We're, uh, just friends. He seemed to need some help tonight, and I didn't want to spend Christmas Eve alone, so I came along."

"Not too many men can quiet a baby like that." Elaine took the teakettle off the stove and picked up some napkins from a holder on the counter. "If your husband has taken off, I wouldn't turn my back on somebody like Russ."

"According to Steve, Russ isn't interested in settling down with one woman."

"Ah." Elaine nodded. "I figured there had to be something wrong with such a perfect guy. Well, then, you don't need him, no matter how great he looks or how good he is with babies. I'm through with trying to change a guy's mind about commitment. That's how I got into this fix."

"No kidding. I'm going to be very careful from now on."

"Yeah. Just treat him the way guys treat us. Have fun but don't lose your heart."

"Elaine, that's probably the best advice I've had in a long time." Jo hoped she could follow it. The longer she was around Russ, the less she felt in possession of her heart.

"If you'll bring the mugs and teabags, we'll take this in by the tree," Elaine said. "You know, I'm beginning to feel as if it's Christmas, after all!"

9

Jo WATCHED with amusement as Russ sat in a rocking chair holding a mug of raspberry-orange decaf tea with one hand while cradling the sleeping baby in his other arm. She'd bet he was sweating under the jacket, but nobody dared ease him out of it because Amanda's cheek was resting firmly against the sheepskin.

"Shall I open the present now or in the morning?" Elaine asked.

"That's up to you," Russ said as he rocked gently back and forth.

"Back home we always opened presents on Christmas Eve," Elaine said.

Jo glanced toward the tree, where five gifts, including the one they'd brought, lay under its meager branches. For decorations Elaine had pasted together a construction-paper chain, strung popcorn and cranberries, and spray-painted pinecones in an obvious attempt to decorate without spending much money.

"The gifts are mostly for Amanda," Elaine said. "One's for Bill and me, and I almost put it away because it makes me mad to look at it, but more packages seemed more festive, so I left it there." She glanced at Jo and Russ. "Would you mind if I opened everything now? This is probably the biggest celebration I'll have."

"Go right ahead," Jo said. "In fact, stay right there and

I'll bring them to you." She set down her mug and walked over to the tree to gather up the gifts.

Elaine sank back against the sofa cushions with her mug of tea. "You can't imagine how much this means to me. I'm feeling positively pampered."

"It's Christmas," Jo said, handing her the small stack of presents. "You should feel pampered."

"I'll save Steve and Claire's for last." Elaine opened a package from her sister containing bibs for Amanda, another that was a small teddy bear from her brother, and a larger package that turned out to be a colorful crib-mobile from her parents. "They wanted to drive out here sometime during Christmas," she said, lining up the presents on the coffee table. "But I haven't told them about Bill leaving, so I talked them out of it."

"I can understand that," Jo said. She couldn't very well lecture somebody about truthfulness, and Russ didn't seem inclined to offer any advice to Elaine, either.

"Guess I'll open the one for Bill and me."

"Just forget his name's on it," Jo said.

"That's a good idea." Elaine slipped her finger under the tape so the paper wouldn't tear as she unwrapped a five-by-seven picture frame. "It's...oh, my. It's of my parents." She held it out in front of her for a moment before clutching it to her chest, her eyes swimming. "I miss them something awful. But I'm afraid they'll say I told you so if they find out the truth. They were really against my marrying Bill."

Jo put a hand on her arm. "Maybe you could call and say you were thinking of breaking up with him. If they go ballistic, you could back off, but if they sound understanding, you could start clueing them in on the situation, little by little."

"That will take a powerful lot of time," Russ said. "Wouldn't it be easier to get it over with all at once?"

Elaine sniffed and shook her head. "I'm not up to that. But Jo's way...I might try that. Thanks. I'm tired of pretending."

"I'm sure you are. And I have a feeling things will work out." Jo put her arms around Elaine and gave her a hug.

"Things will work out," she repeated. "You have Amanda, and a new year is coming up." She released Elaine and they smiled at each other. Then something prompted Jo to look across at Russ.

He'd stopped rocking and was gazing at her intently, as if trying to work through a very knotty problem.

For an unguarded moment she allowed him to see into her heart. Perhaps he should know how he was beginning to affect her. He already knew how she responded to him sexually. Maybe he needed to know there was more to it than that now. If he turned and ran, she'd back off before it was too late to save herself.

He didn't flinch, didn't look away. A slow, steady flame burned in the depths of his dark eyes, and that flame kindled an answering one in Jo. Her focus narrowed to take in only Russ, as if she saw him for the first time. A faint smile curved his mouth, and she wanted to kiss him so much it hurt.

Then Amanda stirred and coughed.

Russ immediately glanced down at the baby and murmured softly to her.

Amanda squirmed and shifted position, her little fist curling over a section of the sheepskin.

"Let's try putting her in the bassinet while you're still here," Elaine said.

"I should probably leave the jacket with you," Russ said as he gradually rose to his feet.

"Of course not," Elaine said. "You'd freeze to death out there."

"Maybe you should open Steve and Claire's present before we put her down," Jo said. "I have a hunch it might help."

"Okay." Elaine carefully took off the ribbon and untied the rattle. "Claire sure knows how to do things right."

"Steve does up the packages," Russ said.

"Really?" Elaine unwrapped the package carefully. "A man who knows how to wrap a present. Now I'm really impressed."

Jo glanced at Russ. "How about you? Did you learn how?"

"Nope. I'm all thumbs."

Jo doubted it. Her experience with Russ had demonstrated great manual dexterity. How she longed to experience it again.

"Oh, this is *beautiful!*" Elaine held up the soft baby blanket crocheted in several shades of pink, from cotton-candy pale to lollipop bright. She held it to her cheek. "This might substitute for your jacket liner, after all. Claire made this, didn't she?"

Russ nodded. "She's keepin' in practice. Oh, and I'm to tell you she'll baby-sit whenever you need her to."

"That sounds wonderful." Elaine sighed. "I know she really wants a baby of her own. Have they thought about adopting a child?"

"They filled out the papers, but it takes time before anything can happen."

"If anybody deserves a baby, it's Steve and Claire," Elaine said.

"That's a fact."

"Well, let's wrap Amanda in this soft blanket and see if it doesn't send her right back into dreamland." As Elaine stood, an envelope dropped to the floor.

"Elaine?" Jo picked up the sealed envelope with Elaine's name written on it. "This was in the package."

"A Christmas card, too. How nice." Elaine took the envelope and opened it. As she scanned the message inside the card, she began to grin. "Well, how about that?"

"How about what?" Russ asked.

Elaine closed the card and slipped it back into the envelope. Then she tucked it into the pocket of her jeans as if to make sure the message remained private. "Oh, nothing. Just a private little joke." She glanced at Russ. "You know, this is turning out to be a pretty good Christmas, after all."

Russ was curious about what had been written in the card that was so secret he couldn't know about it. He'd been given a card for Lucile, too, and there might have been a private message in the cooler meant for Ned and Sharon, for all he knew. He'd ask Steve about it tomorrow morning. If Steve and Claire had just wished everybody a merry Christmas in the note, then it wouldn't be something to keep private, now, would it? Something was up, and Russ wanted to know what it was.

But Elaine wasn't talking as she carefully eased Amanda away from him and wrapped the baby in her new blanket.

Amanda woke up and stared at him, but she didn't start crying again. As Russ gazed into those china-blue eyes, the strangest thing happened.

He'd been thinking how nice it would be to finally have Elaine take her baby back, but now that the moment was here, he wanted to hold that little kid again, wanted to rock her, watch her fingers curl around his jacket and listen to her soft breathing. If he stayed single, he'd never look into his own baby's eyes, because he'd never be a father. That hadn't bothered him before, but it bothered him now.

"I'll just be a minute," Elaine said. "Look, she's drifting off again. Looks like you did the trick, Russ."

"Glad to help."

Crooning softly to Amanda, Elaine carried her into the bedroom.

"You did well with the baby." Jo got up from the couch. "Have you held a lot of them?"

"Not a lot. I've held some. But livin' on a ranch, you're around babies all the time—chicks, kittens, puppies, calves, foals, and once Claire took in some orphaned possums. Baby people aren't any different from baby animals. They just want to feel safe."

"Babies aren't the only ones who want that."

The look in her eyes was the same one she'd given him a few minutes ago, the one that twisted his heart and made him want to hold her and make her feel safe. For a little while there he'd thought how nice that would be, but then he'd reminded himself that he was the one guy a woman should never trust. "Too bad there ain't such a thing," he said.

The warmth slowly left her eyes. "What happened to make you so cynical, Russ?"

"I'm just bein' realistic, is all."

"Then why cuddle kittens and babies?" She sounded impatient. "Why not let them cry and find out early that the world is a big, bad place?"

"That's probably what I should do. Trouble is, I can't."

"Of course you can't." She drew closer. "Because you're a big softie who worries about kittens getting cold and horses needing treats and babies having tummyaches."

He didn't appreciate that assessment. "Don't go gettin' the wrong idea about me, Jo. I'm an ornery cuss. Just ask Steve if you don't—"

"I don't believe it."

The look in her eyes begged him to hold her. "Don't get stuck on me, Jo. You'd be better off stayin' clean away from me, as a matter of fact."

Her green eyes became stormy. "Believe me, I've tried."

"Then try harder." He took hold of her left hand and held it up in front of her face. "For better or worse, you're married. I'm not the answer to that problem."

"You're part of the problem."

"Now wait a minute. All I did was—"

"You cuddled me when I needed it, just like those kittens, just like that baby, and it was wonderful. Then you walked away. You wouldn't have done that to an animal in need. Why did you do it to me?"

He grabbed her by the arms. "Doggone it, woman, I—"

"Amanda's asleep," Elaine said as she walked into the living room. "I can't tell you how much I—whoops. I can go back in there."

Russ released Jo and backed away. "It's okay. We were just…talking."

"Right," Jo said. "We were just figuring where we'd go next." She turned to Russ. "Weren't we?"

Russ adjusted the brim of his Stetson. "Yep."

Elaine didn't look convinced. "My mistake. Well, I'd

better let you two get on with your rounds. I've kept you here long enough."

Russ couldn't get to the door quick enough. This evening was getting out of hand.

"Merry Christmas," Jo called to Elaine as they headed out.

"Yeah, Merry Christmas," Russ added over his shoulder without breaking stride.

"The same to both of you. It's been a real treat." Elaine closed the door after them.

"My God, you're positively running!" Jo sounded out of breath and far behind him.

"We've got a lot to do."

"Bull. You're afraid of me."

"Nope. Just in a hurry." Russ walked up to Blackie and fed the horse a few more carrot chunks. By then Jo had reached the sleigh, and Russ was too much of a gentleman to watch her climb in by herself. He helped her in, although he made his mind a perfect blank when he touched her.

Jo settled herself in the seat. "I say you are afraid of me. I say you were afraid of me back in November."

"You're just makin' me nervous because you're married, that's all." He climbed in and pulled on his gloves.

"What if I wasn't?"

Russ had always hated hypothetical questions. "You are, and that's that. To be honest, I think it'd be a real good idea if I took you home." He picked up the reins and slapped them against Blackie's rump.

"I've got the list, and I know who's next on it."

Cursing, he remembered he'd never taken it back after he handed it to her. "Then I guess you'd best give it to me."

"Nope."

"Come on, Jo. Where is it?"

"You'll have to search me to get it, and I hid it real well."

Wouldn't he love to do that. He'd make a real thorough search and enjoy every second. "Look, sweetheart, I think you've about made up your mind to break your weddin' vows, and the way things are going, I'm liable to weaken and help you do it. I don't want to live with that, so just give me the list and I'll take you home."

"So you've never taken a married woman to bed?"

"Not that I know of. I suppose a woman could have lied to me once or twice, but I never did it on purpose."

"But now you're afraid you might with me. Why would that be?"

Russ ground his teeth in frustration. "Doggone if I know. You're put together real nice, but then so are lots of women. I get a kick out of talkin' to you, but I've talked to others just as easy. There's no blessed reason why you've been sticking in my mind like a burr since November. No reason why I can't—"

"Since November?"

Well, damn. Now he'd gone and done it.

She latched on to his arm. "I've been stuck in your mind like a burr since November?"

He stared straight ahead, concentrating on driving the sleigh. Damn, he never should have said that. He didn't know what was wrong with him. "Off and on."

"Off and on. I don't know what that means."

"We'd best drop this subject, Jo. Who's next on the list? I'll take you home after we make the next delivery." He figured she'd have to take out the list after that, and he'd get it back from her then.

"Hector Barnes is next. We're supposed to just leave the package by the front door."

"Hector Barnes." Russ shook his head. "I didn't know he was still around. He lives near the elementary school Steve and I went to. He used to run us off his property if we stepped one toe on it. I'll bet he's still doin' it, too. I wonder why Steve's givin' him somethin'." He headed down the street that would take him toward the school.

"Maybe it's a big lump of coal."

"No, Steve and Claire don't do that. The presents are always somethin' nice."

"Well, enough about Hector Barnes. I want to know what you meant when you said I've been stuck like a burr in your mind off and on for the past month."

He sighed. She wasn't going to let the subject drop, so he might as well try to give her an answer. "Naturally I thought about you once in a while. We had us quite a time that night."

"You said like a burr. A burr is something folks usually aren't happy about."

"Once I heard you were married, I wasn't happy thinkin' about somebody who was off limits. I tried not to."

"But you did, anyway."

"Some." *Every night, and sometimes when the action was slow during the day, too. He'd acted like a damn fool.*

"I was so sure you put me right out of your mind the minute you left town. I figured by sundown the next day you were wrapped around some other cowgirl."

The unfairness of that finally stirred his anger.

"You must be measurin' me by your yardstick, honey. I'm not the one who ran off to Vegas and got myself married."

Her voice grew quiet. "I thought for sure you'd go find somebody else in no time."

He didn't say anything. Lord knows he'd already said too much.

"You left because the night meant too much, didn't you? You left because of what you were starting to feel about me, didn't you?"

"Makes no difference."

"It does if I'm not married."

He'd about had it with that reasoning. "It doesn't work that way, Jo. You don't just decide. You stood in front of a preacher, or whoever does the ceremony in Vegas, and now it's a legal thing. You have to undo it legally, too."

"I didn't stand up in front of a preacher. I'm not married. I made it up."

He just about fell off the seat. Then he hauled back on the reins. "Whoa, Blackie! Whoa, boy!" When the sleigh crunched to a stop, he turned to Jo. "What did you say?"

She looked nervous, but she met his gaze. "I made it up. I'm not really married."

"You're not?" He didn't believe her for a minute. Sexual frustration could make people tell all sorts of stories.

"No." She looked so adorable with her Santa hat perched on her head. "So you don't have to feel guilty about wanting me. You're not breaking any of your rules."

"Now, isn't that convenient."

"You don't believe me."

"No, sweetheart, I don't. I'd like to, and that's a fact. But you're only trying to ease my conscience and make the evening more interesting for both of us. I appreciate that, but I can't oblige you." He clucked to Blackie and the sleigh moved down the road again.

"But I'm not really married! I'll prove it to you." She took off her gold band and threw it into a snowbank.

Russ pulled back on the reins again and stopped the sleigh. "You'd best go get that. The snow's packed pretty hard, and it might not have sunk down too far."

"I don't care about it. It only reminds me of Tommy, anyway. Good riddance."

He turned to her. "Who the hell is Tommy?"

"My ex-husband."

"Another husband?" Russ was beginning to wonder if this woman had husbands stashed everywhere.

"No, the only one I ever had. He left a year ago, on the Friday night after Thanksgiving. That was what I was trying to forget the night I...took you home with me."

Russ became more confused by the minute. "So the ring that Richard gave you reminds you of Tommy?"

"Richard didn't give me a ring."

"He made you use the same ring you had from your first marriage? Now if that isn't the cheapest, meanest, sorriest—"

"Richard didn't give me a ring because Richard doesn't exist! I made him up and put Tommy's ring back on!"

He stared at her. "Honey, you are one terrific woman in bed, and you're fun to be with, but I'm beginning to think you need a head doctor."

She stared right back at him. "You could be absolutely right. Only a crazy person would get herself into a fix like this. So you don't believe that I made up this husband of mine?"

"No, I reckon I don't. I think you're just tired of being married to somebody who doesn't give you any satisfaction, and it's Christmas, so you're feeling extra lonely, and I'm handy."

Jo sighed. "It sure is Christmas, and it's absolutely true that Richard's given me no satisfaction whatsoever, and we still have presents to deliver. I guess we'd better get on with it."

"Are you gonna go fetch that ring?"

"No, I'm not. But trust me, it won't be a problem."

"I'm not surprised, to tell the truth. If he's not man enough to do right by you, he won't be man enough to make you dig through that snowbank to get his ring."

"If it was your ring, you'd make me dig for it?"

"For as long as it took, honey. But then, if it was my ring, you wouldn't be throwing it in the first place."

10

JO HAD REALLY outsmarted herself, coming up with this marriage story. She'd imagined she could reveal her true status whenever she wanted and change everything. She'd thought Russ might be upset that she'd tricked him, but she hadn't imagined that he just plain wouldn't believe her new story.

But he didn't. He figured she was simply so frustrated by her jerk of a husband that she was trying to fool Russ into going to bed with her. His reaction had given her time to reconsider whether it was wise to try to convince him, even assuming she could succeed. And in the meantime, they had a job to do.

Russ drove past the empty schoolyard and up to a house with absolutely no Christmas decorations. Only the flashing of a television screen visible through the front window gave any color to the house, and no lights burned at all. The sidewalk had been shoveled, but otherwise the place looked almost deserted.

"I take it Hector Barnes doesn't honor the season," Jo said.

"Never did. Used to call up the school and complain because he could hear kids singing Christmas carols on the playground."

"Maybe it's a religious thing."

"No, the principal asked, according to what I heard. Hector said he didn't belong to any particular religion, but he had no use for Christmas and even less use for kids."

"And he lives right close to a school. How strange."

"Steve said we're supposed to leave this by the front door?"

"That's what it said on the list." She knew better than to get the piece of paper. Once he got his hands on it again, he might decide to take her home. She wasn't ready for that to happen yet, and if she had to use the list against him, she would.

Russ climbed down. "Maybe you'd better stay in the sleigh. No tellin' how Hector's gonna act if he hears somebody on his front porch."

"Nonsense. This is the very time I should come with you. He won't be nearly as suspicious if both of us go to the door."

"I don't know about that."

"I'm coming with you, Russ."

"Okay, if you have to." He hoisted her down and released her immediately. Then he went to the back of the sleigh and took out a bulky package.

"What do you think it is?"

"Something soft and squishy."

"I'm dying to know what it is."

"We're not stayin' to find out. Keep behind me, okay?"

Jo grew a little less sure of herself. "Could this be one of those times we get shot at?"

"I don't think so. He always yelled at us about havin' a shotgun, but nobody ever saw one. I think he was mostly blowin' smoke."

"Why did he yell at you? Did you do stuff to him?"

"Why, sure we did. Somebody acting like an old grouch just riles kids up all the more. We threw eggs and tee-peed his front yard more times than I can count. Steve was the worst. Funny how walking up to his house still scares the devil out of me."

"It's spooky with no decorations and no lights except for the television screen."

"You can go back anytime you want."

"Nope. I'm in."

"Am I supposed to ring the doorbell?"

Jo thought about the instructions she'd read. "No. Just leave the package by the front door, where he'll find it in the morning, was what the instructions were."

"Good. Maybe he'll never know we were here." Russ stepped on the sagging wooden steps and they creaked. "Damn. Stay off the—"

"Too late," Jo said as she followed him up, the steps squeaking with every movement she made.

"Then let's get the hell out of here," Russ said, dumping the package by the door and grabbing Jo's hand as he started back down the steps.

Jo's foot hit a patch of ice as she started after Russ, and if he hadn't been holding her hand she would have fallen. Instead, her ankle twisted underneath her, and she cried out.

"Jo?" Russ grabbed her by both elbows.

"I'm okay." Her ankle hurt like hell, but she wasn't going to tell him that. "Let's go."

The door of the house banged open. "Whoever's out there, I have a shotgun pointed right at your heart!"

"I'm gonna kill Steve," Russ muttered, shoving Jo behind him as he faced the porch. "Merry Christmas, Mr. Barnes. We left a package for you there by the door. We'll be goin' now."

"The hell you will! Come closer so I can see who you

are. A package, indeed. Probably one of them stink bombs."

Russ didn't budge. "No, sir, it's a present from Steve and Claire Gibson."

Jo peeked around his arm, but she couldn't see much except a dim outline of a thin man standing in the darkened doorway. She couldn't tell if he was holding a shotgun or not.

"Steve Gibson?" Hector snorted. "That hooligan giving me a present? That'll be the day! And who're you? Santy Claus?"

"I'm his little brother, Russ."

"Oh, yeah. I remember you, too, you little twerp, picking up bad habits from all the older kids. I'm surprised you and your brother aren't in jail someplace."

"Steve turned out real good, but you're right about me. I probably should be in jail by now. Have a good holiday, Mr. Barnes." Russ started to turn around.

"Wait! You're not going anywhere until I open this thing. If it's going to explode or spray me with something, I want you still in the neighborhood when I call the cops."

"Oh, for crying out loud." Russ blew out a breath. "I'll do better than that. I'll come up on your porch, so I'll get the same treatment meant for you." He turned to Jo. "Stay here."

"In your dreams."

"Jo—"

"I've been dying to know what's in that package. Now get going." Despite the throbbing pain in her ankle, she followed him back up the walk, being careful not to limp.

"You got a bulb in that porch light of yours?" Russ asked as he mounted the steps.

"Nope. Don't need one. I got all the light I need inside, and I don't care if people on the outside can see or not."

"What a sweetheart," Jo murmured, joining Russ on the porch.

"So you're gonna unwrap this exploding present in the dark?" Russ asked.

As the shadowy figure in the doorway remained silent, only the voices from the television could be heard. "Guess I'll have to take it inside," Hector said at last.

"Good. Then we'll be leaving," Russ said.

"No. You come in, too. Just don't touch anything."

"Look, Mr. Barnes, we really have to be—"

"We'd be glad to come in," Jo said, giving Russ a little shove forward. She'd heard something in Hector's voice, a faint note of eagerness at the prospect of having company.

Besides, she really wanted to see what Steve and Claire had picked out for this guy.

With the bulky package under one arm, Hector walked inside. He flicked a wall switch and a lamp came on beside the sofa. "Shut the door behind you. Don't need to heat the neighborhood."

Jo didn't think the neighborhood would get very warm from the heat in this house. Hector had on a heavy sweatshirt with the hood pulled up and what must have been two layers of sweatpants, judging from how thick his legs looked in relation to his thin hands and face. Jo figured his age to be anywhere between sixty and ninety, but his eyes were the eyes of Methuselah.

The furnishings in the living room were sparse, but everything seemed spotless, including the dozens of framed pictures that covered the walls and every flat surface. Jo quickly realized they were all of the same person, beginning when he was a little boy and working up to a faded eight-by-ten color photograph of him as a young man in uniform.

Hector didn't ask them to sit down or offer any refreshment. He just stood holding his present and gazing at it.

"Where do you keep that shotgun, Mr. Barnes?" Russ asked.

"What?" Hector glanced up at Russ.

"I don't see a shotgun leanin' by the front door."

"Oh. It's not...there."

No shotgun, Jo decided, and relaxed a little. "Aren't you going to open your present?"

"It's probably a big package of toilet paper, just like the kind I had to pick off the bushes when you hooligans used to tee-pee the house."

"One way to find out." Russ shifted his weight and fiddled with the zipper on his coat.

"I guess so." Hector seemed to be prolonging the surprise.

Jo wondered if he was secretly savoring the chance to open a present for the first time in years. As Hector slowly began to undo the wrapping, Jo watched in fascination as a large teddy bear emerged. She couldn't think of a single thing less appropriate for a man like Hector.

Hector stared at the stuffed animal. He opened his mouth a couple of times, as if to say something, but apparently he was struck dumb by the strangeness of the gift. "It's a joke, right?" he said. "They're making fun of me."

Russ looked as puzzled as Hector. "Steve and Claire never do that at Christmas. They always try real hard to give people somethin' they can use."

"And they thought I could use a teddy bear?"

Jo caught sight of a sealed envelope tied with a ribbon to the bear's paw. "Maybe they explain it in the card," she said.

Holding the bear in one arm, Hector untied the ribbon and opened the card. It was an awkward maneuver, one he could have accomplished better by putting down the bear.

Then Jo realized he was enjoying the feel of the stuffed toy. Maybe this wasn't such a dumb gift, after all. She remembered the big panda she'd had as a little girl, and how many times she'd drawn comfort from hugging that soft body. People didn't necessarily outgrow that need, especially if they were all alone.

Her gaze met Russ's. He must have been thinking the same thoughts, because he smiled at her. She smiled back. Another Christmas success. The moment grew as understanding flowed between them. Then the current changed to something far more erotic, and Jo decided she'd better return her attention to Hector.

Hector's lips moved as he read the message inside the card. "Huh," he said, glancing at Russ. Then he read the card again.

"Does the note explain the present?" Jo asked.

"Kind of." All the belligerence had gone out of Hector's voice. "Well, I'd have to say it does."

"Why did they give you the bear?" Russ asked.

Hector tucked the card back inside the envelope before looking at Russ. "Alan always did love Christmas," he said.

"Excuse me?" Russ looked bewildered.

"Is Alan the person in the pictures?" Jo asked gently.

Hector's gaze swept the room, and what was almost a smile touched his face. "Yes, that's my Alan."

She didn't need any more information to know that

Alan had died, probably in the military, and Hector had
completely closed down. No more Christmases, no more
joy, no more delight in children. He'd scuttled back so
far into his cave, that people weren't welcome. Even a
pet would have been too much of an intrusion. But a
stuffed bear offered comfort without making any demands.

The way Hector was holding on to that bear, Jo didn't
think he'd put it down for quite a while. Gradually she
became aware that the opening of *It's a Wonderful Life*
was playing on television.

She took a chance and gestured toward the set. "I
watch that movie every Christmas Eve."

Hector peered at the television as if he'd forgotten it
was turned on. "Oh, yeah." He grabbed a remote. "Sure
don't need that claptrap on."

"Don't turn it off just yet," Jo said. "Watch a little of it.
It's a great movie."

With the remote in one hand and the bear still
clutched in his other arm, Hector looked at her.

"I really recommend it," Jo said.

"Yeah, and who are you, anyway?" Hector said.

"She's with me," Russ said, coming over to put an
arm around Jo.

Boy, how she loved hearing that from Russ, with that
note of pride in his voice. She loved his arm around her
even more. It made the throbbing in her ankle seem un-
important.

Hector shrugged. "Whatever."

"We'd best be going," Russ said.

"Whatever," Hector said again.

Russ guided Jo toward the door. "Merry Christmas,
Mr. Barnes," he said over his shoulder.

"Try the movie," Jo said, trying not to limp. She noticed he hadn't switched channels yet.

"I might. Then again, I might not. Close the door tight on your way out."

When the door was closed behind them and they were standing on the front porch, Russ kept his arm around Jo and gave her a little squeeze. "You were great in there. I think he's gonna watch that movie."

"I hope so. Nobody should live that way. He might as well be dead."

"That was his son in all those pictures, wasn't it?"

Jo turned her face up to his. "Had to be. Did you see the way he was holding on to the teddy bear?"

"Like he didn't want to ever let go." His grip tightened a fraction. "I know exactly how he feels."

Her breath caught at the tenderness in his expression.

"You do make it tough on a guy," Russ murmured. Then he dipped his head and gave her a gentle kiss.

She held perfectly still to absorb the magic as his mouth caressed hers with restrained passion.

He lifted his lips a fraction and his breath tickled her face. "I don't know what it is about you, lady, but I can't seem to stay away."

Warmth sluiced through her as she breathed in an intoxicating mixture of leather and aftershave. "Then don't."

"I sure never expected to be kissin' a woman on old man Barnes's front porch, either." His lips were hungrier this time, his message more intimate.

She moaned softly and turned into his embrace.

"Break it up, you two," called Hector from the doorway. "What sort of place do you think this is, carrying on like that?"

They separated and turned toward the door where

Hector stood scowling at them while he held tight to his teddy bear.

"I don't allow necking on my property," Hector muttered, but his disapproving statement lost some of its punch when he delivered it holding on to a stuffed animal.

"I could have sworn there was some mistletoe tacked up there in the rafters," Russ said.

"You know better than that! No mistletoe around this place!"

Russ grinned at him. "Maybe next year. Come on, Jo. Let's go find us some mistletoe."

"Merry Christmas, Mr. Barnes," Jo called as Russ led her down the steps. "And a Happy New—oh." She grimaced as she accidentally put all her weight on her bad ankle. "Happy New Year!" she finished brightly, trying to pretend nothing had happened.

The door closed behind them as Russ turned back to her. "Something's wrong with you, isn't it? Did you twist your ankle before?"

"I'm fine. Let's just go."

He released her hand. "Go ahead. I want to watch you walk, if everything's so perfectly fine."

"It is." She started out bravely. "See? I'm—oh!" Pain sliced through her ankle as if somebody had jabbed a knife into it.

Russ stepped forward and scooped her into his arms. "Oh, you're just fine, all right. You sprained the heck out of your ankle, didn't you? And you weren't going to tell me."

"I'm afraid you'll take me home. I don't want to go home, Russ."

He headed for the sleigh. "We'll talk about that in a minute."

"Then let's talk about you kissing me." Being carried in his arms reminded her of the time he'd carried her into her bedroom. Maybe it was worth spraining an ankle to get held close like this. "Do you believe me now? That I made up the story about being married? I figured it was the best way to keep me from doing something stupid like that again, but now I realize that you're different than I thought, and—"

"We'll talk about all that later." He reached the sleigh and lowered her carefully to the ground. "Hold on to the side of the sleigh while I clear you a space in the back."

"Russ, I don't want—"

His kiss, firm and thorough, ended her protest. "Now be quiet, Jo."

"Okay." If he'd keep on kissing her like that, she'd be willing to take a vow of complete silence.

"We only have two more stops to make, anyway." He hoisted the remaining packages out of the back and carried them around to Jo's side of the front seat. Then he grabbed the blankets she'd been wrapping up in and tossed them in the sleigh bed.

"Does that mean you'll let me ride along while you make the last two deliveries?"

He folded one blanket and laid it in the bed of the sleigh. "I'll decide that after I take a look at that ankle."

She leaned closer. "I'm sure you could kiss it and make it better," she said in a deliberately sultry tone.

He glanced up from his task of arranging the blankets into a nest for her. "Don't think I haven't thought of it."

"That's nice to know."

"I swear, woman, you'd be able to break down the resolutions of a saint, and I ain't no saint."

"Glad to hear it. I don't much care for saints, myself."

He gave the blankets a final adjustment and walked

back around the sleigh. "Well, I'm about as far from that as you can imagine. Now lean on me and I'll try to hoist you in without disturbin' your ankle too much."

"I can probably climb in. In fact, I could probably ride in front."

He took her in his strong arms. "Lean, woman. Let me do the maneuverin' and just go with my movement."

"I like the sound of that." She relaxed against him.

"Damnation." He got his arm under her hips. "You make a man think of nothin' but..."

"But what?"

"I'm sure you know." With a groan of effort he lifted her over the edge of the sleigh bed and laid her gently in the nest of blankets. "There." He doubled a section of blanket and used great care to position her ankle on it. "I'll try not to hit any bumps."

"Do you need to know who the next gift goes to?"

"Nope. We're gettin' away from Hector's, and then I'm gonna take a look at the damage before we go any further. The next stop after that might be the emergency room."

"I don't need an emergency room," Jo called after him as he climbed up to the seat of the sleigh. *I need you*, she whispered into the darkness.

11

RUSS'S THOUGHTS zigzagged like a jackrabbit as he guided Blackie down the snowpacked road. He chose the route with as much care as possible so as not to make the ride too rough on Jo. Up ahead was a little side lane that led to a dead end and some hiking trails. He could pull off there and take time to check Jo's ankle. With no hazard lights on the sleigh, he didn't want to stop someplace where they could get rear-ended in the dark.

And what else do you want to take time for, son? his conscience asked him. Damned if he hadn't started believing that Jo might not be married, that she might have made up that husband of hers, like she said. It sounded as if she'd done it to keep herself from sleeping with him again, which made as much sense as the other possibility—that a woman like Jo would hitch up with a loser who'd leave her alone on Christmas.

Nothing about Jo made a lot of sense to him, to be honest. But then, he probably didn't make much sense to her, either. He didn't know the demons driving her, and she sure as hell didn't know the ones driving him. She'd sworn to him that she wasn't married, and she'd thrown away her wedding ring. Teetering on the edge of temptation as he was, those actions were enough to send him crashing into hell. But maybe it wasn't even a sin.

The first order of business was finding out just how bad she'd hurt herself on that patch of ice. Hector Barnes would do well to put a lightbulb in the fixture on his front porch and shovel his steps better. Living like that was dangerous to Hector and dangerous to other folks, too.

Still, Russ couldn't work up the same anger toward the old man that he'd enjoyed as a kid. The world had taken away the most important thing in Hector's life, and he'd built a wall to keep people from his private heartache. Russ had no trouble understanding that.

Looking at Hector was like looking in a fun-house mirror, and Russ wasn't all that happy with what he saw. He had a powerful need to get that image out of his head. Kissing Jo sure did the trick. In fact, being with Jo seemed to get rid of those devils running around in his mind. It wasn't a permanent solution, of course, but it was nice while it lasted.

He spied the lane and turned Blackie's head so they cruised right into it with scarcely a ripple in the ride. Pine branches heavy with snow reached out over the roadway, turning it into a cozy little spot. Reining Blackie to a halt, Russ discovered his pulse jumping the same way it used to back in the days when he'd search out these darkened lanes with a girl in the truck seat next to him.

They were stopping to check Jo's ankle, he reminded himself as he vaulted down from the sleigh and negoti-ated a couple of drifts to get to Jo. He'd propped her up against the back of the sleigh with both legs out straight and the injured ankle elevated a little. She was nearly hidden in the shadows caused by the tall trees surround-ing them, but he had an excellent memory of how she'd looked lying there, as if she was expecting something nice from him.

"How was the ride?" he asked. "I tried to take it easy."

"The ride was fine," she said. "You're making too much of this. It's a slight sprain, is all."

"Let's find out." He climbed carefully into the sleigh. There was just enough room for him to kneel beside her. He pulled off his gloves and laid them in the sleigh bed. "Now stop me if I hurt you. I'm gonna take off your boot, first."

"And what are you going to take off after that?" she said softly.

Beneath his jeans, stirrings began. "Now, Jo, don't be sayin' such things and distractin' me. You could be hurt bad."

"Nope. Some torn ligaments. That's it."

"You wouldn't admit it if your ankle was broken clean through." He found the zipper on the side of her boot and eased it down. "Does that hurt?" Her floral scent reached out to him, teasing him to come closer.

"No, it doesn't hurt. Russ, I'm not married. I'm really not."

"So that's your story, and you're stickin' to it." He worked the boot off slowly, all the while thinking about the last time he'd taken off her boots and the sweet loving that had followed.

"I'm not asking you to help me cheat. I wouldn't do that."

"I'd like to believe you, Jo." He drew off her wool sock.

"You can believe me. And I should warn you, I've hidden the list," she said.

"Is that right?" Cradling her heel, he gently pushed her sweatpant cuff up over the slight swelling in her ankle. The boot had probably helped keep it down. "I suppose you're not gonna tell me where?"

"Not if you're thinking of taking me home."

He smiled to himself. He was beginning to cherish that stubborn streak of hers. Married or not, she was a challenge he enjoyed. "That's probably where you should be, at home with this ankle propped up on a pillow."

"Then I guess you'll have to search for the list before you take me home."

"And where would I be searchin' for it?" As if he didn't know. He ran his fingers lightly over her ankle.

"Let's just say I'm keeping that list very warm."

Lord, he could imagine where she'd tucked that piece of paper, right next to her soft skin, maybe between her breasts, or even between her thighs. He sucked in a breath. "Sweetheart, you're makin' it hard for me to concentrate."

"That's because you're concentrating on the wrong thing."

Forcing himself to ignore the invitation in her voice and the pictures it painted in his mind, he probed her ankle with caution. "Does that hurt?"

"Not too much. You could make me forget all about my ankle, you know."

"Jo. Now quit." It took all his willpower not to start taking off the rest of her clothes. At least she wasn't yelling as he touched her ankle. If she'd been hurt really bad, she wouldn't be able to stand the pressure he was putting on it. He held her foot, massaging it gently while he thought about what to do.

"If you're so worried about my ankle, we could probably figure out a way to use snow to make an ice pack," she said.

The minute she made the suggestion, he realized he had the perfect thing in his wallet. No wonder he'd thought of it, considering the way his mind was working. But if he made it into an ice pack, he couldn't use it for its intended purpose. Maybe a guardian angel was keeping him from heeding the devil's call.

"In fact, you do have something we could use for an ice pack," she said.

He sighed and decided he'd allow himself to be saved from the flames, although they did look tempting. "Yeah, I do."

"See, I don't need an emergency room. We can wrap an ice pack around my ankle and make the last two deliveries just fine."

"That's right, little darlin', we sure can." He reached in his hip pocket and pulled out his wallet. As he took the condom out of it and started to slip his wallet back in his pocket, Jo grabbed his arm.

"What is that?" she asked, leaning forward to see what was in his hand.

"It's gonna be your ice pack."

She started to laugh.

"Yeah, it might seem funny, but it'll work. This is a real good brand and shouldn't leak or anything. Nobody will see it, anyhow, if you're worried about bein' embarrassed. We'll wind your scarf around your ankle and pull your sock over that."

She was laughing so hard she barely got the words out. "Is that the only one you have?"

"Yeah, but one will be enough until we get to your house."

She choked back another burst of laughter and cleared her throat. "That all depends, now, doesn't it?"

"On what?"

She grasped the collar of his coat and pulled him toward her. Her voice grew low and seductive. "Russ, that isn't what I had in mind when I mentioned making an ice pack."

Her warm breath against his face drove him wild as the flames of temptation flickered to life and began to scorch him all over again. "It...wasn't?"

"No, you sexy cowhand. I was talking about the plastic bag you used to hold Blackie's carrots."

He grinned. "Oh." Then as he realized what that meant, his heart started pounding. She could be married, and he could be sending himself to the devil for loving her. He angled his head and leaned closer, his lips almost on hers. "I guess that would work, too, wouldn't it?"

She ran her finger along his lower lip. "I think they would both work...in different ways."

He combed his fingers through her hair and cupped the back of her head. He might be willing to walk into hell for one more chance to make love to her, but she had to answer for it, too. "Lady, do you know what you're saying?"

"I'm saying that I want you to use the carrot bag on my ankle and the other item for loving me six ways to Sunday, right here, right now, cowboy."

"Let's try for seven," he murmured, leaping straight into the fire.

THE BAG OF packed snow numbed Jo's ankle and took away some of the pain, not that she cared much at that point. True to his word, Russ found her clothing no barrier to what he wanted. The layers she'd put on to protect herself against the cold didn't stand a chance against the heat of his exploring caress.

Carefully propping her bandaged ankle on a rolled blanket, he eased her legs apart so that he could kneel between them. Taking off his hat, he leaned down and cradled her face in both hands. "Oh, darlin', how I've missed touching you."

"I've missed touching you, too," she murmured, reaching for the zipper on his heavy sheepskin coat.

"I've missed the feel of your sweet mouth." He kissed her with slow deliberation, working up to the moment he took possession with his tongue.

As he showed her with sensuous strokes how he intended to pleasure her, he opened her coat and pulled up the hem of her sweatshirt. The snaps of her long underwear gave way, and in short order he'd pulled the Christmas list from where she'd tucked it between her breasts.

He lifted his head and smiled down at her. "Found it."

"Does that mean you're finished with the search?"

He tucked the list in his coat pocket. "Nope." With calm precision he continued flipping open snaps. "No tellin' what other secrets you have in there."

She was wearing nothing beneath the long underwear, and the cold night air puckered her nipples. "Keep me warm, Russ," she murmured.

"That's my intention." The heat of his mouth soon drove away the chill. Supporting her with an arm beneath her bottom, he tilted her back just enough so that he could tunnel his fingers through the curls between her thighs. The minute he found the aching nub concealed by those curls, she began to quiver.

She'd never responded to a man so quickly as she did to Russ. As his finger drew a lazy circle over that flashpoint, the tightening deep within her began, as it had on their first night together. He pleasured her breasts and kept up that slow stroking. Her breathing quickened as the pressure grew under that light but persistent touch. He knew just how, and just where, she needed that touch to bring her joy. She began to shake, and finally arched upward with a soft cry of release.

He brought his mouth back to hers, murmuring to her between kisses. "That's it, honey." He pushed his fingers in deep to prolong the moment by caressing her there. "Catch fire for me. I love how you do that."

"It's...the way you...touch me," she said, struggling to catch her breath.

"I hope so. I surely do."

"Russ, I need you," she murmured, cupping the bulge straining the denim of his jeans. "I need you bad."

"And that's real good," he whispered against her mouth.

The ache within her became so fierce that she unfastened his belt and opened his fly to get closer to the source of her satisfaction. He moaned as she rubbed him through the cotton underwear that barely contained him.

Hungry for more, she slid her hand inside his briefs and took a handful of warm, rigid male. He gasped against her mouth. Using both hands, she pushed his underwear down so that she had better access. He began to tremble as she continued stroking him.

Raging need made her bold, and she pulled back from his kiss. "Aren't you cold, too?" she murmured, brushing her thumb over the moist tip of his erection.

"Not even close."

"You must be on a night like this. Rise onto your knees a little more, and let me make you warm, the way you made me warm."

He hesitated. Then with a sigh of surrender, he did as she asked, bracing his hands on the back of the sleigh as she took all that pulsing arousal into her mouth. The sheepskin liner of his coat brushed her cheeks as she loved him, and the loving made her moist and desperate to have that fullness deep inside her.

"Stop, little darlin'," he said between gulps for air. "You're too accomplished at that business for your own good."

She slowly drew back, but kept her hand wrapped around the prize she wanted so desperately. "Give me the condom, Russ. Now."

He fumbled in the pocket of his coat, pulled out the envelope and gave it to her with a trembling hand. "Be careful, sweetheart. You've got me to the boilin' point."

"I won't let you boil over." She opened the package and unrolled the condom over him. "Not yet, anyway."

"Ah, Jo. It'll be soon." He eased down and took off his coat.

"Russ, put that back on! You'll freeze!"

"Not with what I'm about to be doin', I won't." He folded the coat so the sheepskin side was out. "And I need your sweet bottom up a little higher for this next part."

"I can—"

"Not with your ankle, you can't." Scooping an arm under her, he lifted her and shoved the folded coat under her hips. "Now lean back just a little, so I can...there..." His shaft probed between the soft folds of her femininity that parted so easily, giving him entrance. "That's good...oh, little darlin'." He held her hips and pushed home. "Ah, Jo." He groaned and shifted a fraction to slide deeper still. "We do fit real nice."

"Yes..." Her breathing grew shallow. "We do." Her

senses reeled with the beauty of it. She'd wondered if her memory had exaggerated the perfect nature of their joining, but her memory hadn't done this moment justice.

He eased back and snugged in again. "There's been no others since you."

Tremors radiated through her body from the sensitive spot where they were joined. "Not for me, either." As he stroked back and forth again, she whimpered at the glorious sensation. "I need you, Russ. I need this."

His lips were close to her ear as he moved sensuously within her. "How much do you need it, sweetheart?"

"A whole...lot," she whispered.

His breathing became labored as the pace increased. "Would you...cheat for it?"

Through the haze of pleasure created by his sure rhythm, she realized what he was asking. "No," she said, gasping as the tremors began to take her.

"I would, darlin'." He thrust harder, driving her closer toward the edge. "I would do most anything...to get inside you...like this."

"Russ, I'm not... " She lost all speech as a stunning climax exploded in rhythm with his relentless movement. Wave upon wave of pleasure crashed over her, wringing little cries of wonder from her lips.

His voice rasped in her ear. "Most anything at all...ah, Jo. Hold me tight, girl." He groaned and pushed in deep as his body heaved and shuddered against her.

Jo stroked his back as aftershocks quivered through him. As his words echoed in the cold stillness of the winter night, she wondered if he knew how much he'd admitted just now, if he'd ever told anyone else in the world that he needed them that much.

RUSS EXPECTED GUILT to hit him sooner or later, but right now, as he got dressed again and helped Jo button up, he couldn't remember feeling better in his life. He decided not to think past the next couple of hours and just enjoy feeling good for a change. Misery would come to visit him soon enough. It always did.

Maybe it was the happiness coming from Jo that put him in such a great mood. He'd done her right, and this time he could see the results of that. When they'd made love before, he'd cut out before she could let him know how much pleasure he'd given her.

She was letting him know now, all right. While he was tucking her in and arranging the blankets so she'd stay warm during the rest of the ride, she kept smiling as if she couldn't stop.

"You look happy, sweetheart," he said, smiling back because he couldn't help himself.

"I'll tell you something, Russ. Nobody's ever loved me the way you do."

"It's easy." He pulled the heaviest blanket up under her chin. "Only an idiot wouldn't be able to make good love to a woman like you."

She took hold of his collar again to pull him closer. "Then I guess I've been unlucky enough to run into some idiots."

He was beginning to like her getting him by the collar like that and tugging him down so her full lips were only an inch or two away.

"Kiss me once more before we head out, cowboy," she murmured.

He didn't have to be asked twice. Her mouth was one of the wonders of the world, in his opinion. As he enjoyed the soft texture and the exciting taste of her, he remembered how he'd felt when she'd used her mouth to "keep him warm," as she'd said. That was the moment when he'd known he'd give up anything, even his soul, to have her. Just thinking about her tongue and what it could do made him hard again.

He drew away, although he sure didn't want to. "I can't kiss you anymore until we've delivered the last two presents," he murmured. "Or the job won't get done."

"Will you kiss me after we finish the job?"

He brushed his mouth over hers, just once, teasing them both. "Maybe."

She got him back by running her tongue over his lower lip. "Will you take my clothes off again after we finish the job?"

He was getting hot all over again. He'd better climb into the front seat and get on with playing Santa Claus. Still he lingered, dropping a brief kiss on her lips. "Maybe."

"Will you—"

"Yes," he said, giving himself up to one more kiss.

When the pressure against his fly became almost painful, he forced himself to move away from her. He was breathing as if he'd just chased down a runaway horse. "Did you...figure out the next house we're supposed to go to?"

"I think the name was Bobby or Benny or something. That part was smeared. But the address wasn't too far from here."

"Benny Turnbull. He wouldn't be far from here. Steve and Claire laid out the route so there's no doubling back."

"And who's Benny?"

"A little kid. I think he's about five. He came out to the ranch this summer with his dad. I guess his mother—

well, she got into drugs, and they tried all sorts of treatment programs, but nothing took. Finally she left, and the last thing I heard, nobody knew where she was."

"Poor little guy. Poor father, too."

"Yeah. I guess he knows Steve from somewhere, and Steve asked him to bring Benny out and go riding last fall. We have a gelding that's real good with kids. But then the guy had to go to Phoenix, where there was work, and he took Benny. They must be back now."

"Then we'd better get over to Benny's house."

"Right." He started to climb out of the sleigh.

"Oh, how's your ankle feeling?"

"Like I could dance a jig. I think your cure did the trick."

He actually believed that she might not be feeling the pain now. But his "cure" hadn't really fixed her ankle. "Don't be doin' any dancin'. I think you'd best stay right there when we get to Benny's house."

"Only if you promise to come back and check on me after you've delivered the present."

He gazed at her and longed to climb right back under those blankets and start all over again. "You're a temptation, darlin'."

"So are you, cowboy."

Determined to finish his task, he grabbed his gloves and pulled them on as he headed for the front of the sleigh. Before he climbed into the driver's seat, he walked up to Blackie and dug out a few of the carrot chunks that were now rattling around loose in his coat pocket.

"Here you go, boy," he said, feeding the chunks to Blackie. "Lord, I'm glad you can't talk," he murmured. "You must have wondered what in tarnation was goin' on in the back of the sleigh just now, all that bumping around and moaning." He scratched under Blackie's mane. "Thanks for standin' so quietly all through it, son. If you'd taken off, you coulda maimed me for life." With a grin, he patted the horse one more time before returning to the sleigh and swinging up to the driver's seat.

"Got any more Christmas carols?" he asked Jo as he gathered up the reins.

"I have tons of Christmas carols. Which one do you want?"

"You know, I have a hankerin' to hear 'Joy to the World.'"

12

GETTING BACK on the main road was a little trickier than Russ had figured on. He had to drive to the dead end and bring the sleigh around in a half circle to get headed in the right direction. In the process he knew he must have jostled Jo's ankle when the runners hit a bump. She sang through it all.

"You sure you're okay back there?" he called after the second bump.

"I have never been more okay," she hollered.

"Why don't you sing with me, cowboy?"

"What the heck," he muttered to himself. And before he knew it, there he was, driving a sleigh down a snowy road, singing "Joy to the World" right along with Jo. Steve would never have believed such a thing was possible. Blackie swiveled his ears back as if to catch the sound, and his trot grew more brisk, making the bells on his collar jingle merrily in tune with the carols.

When the first tune was finished, they moved on to "Silver Bells" and "Santa Claus Is Coming to Town." It was the first time Russ had tried singing sober in years. The feeling wasn't half-bad, and he could remember the words to the songs a darn sight better than he could when he was drunk.

They were singing "Rudolph, the Red-Nosed Reindeer" when he pulled up in front of Benny's house. He kept it up as he took the two packages addressed to

Benny and climbed down from the sleigh. Then, finishing the chorus with Jo, he walked to where she was, swung up on the running board and leaned over to give her a quick kiss.

"That was fun," she said, grinning at him.

"The singin' or the kissin'?"

"Both. Come back soon, Santa."

"I don't know if I should." Lord, he was having a good time. "Have you been a good little girl?"

"Nope."

"Then I'll get back here as quick as I can. Sounds like you're just the kind of little girl I've been lookin' for."

Her laughter followed him up the walk to the bungalow where father and son lived. She was *exactly* the sort of girl he'd been looking for, he thought as his grin faded. But once she knew the truth about him, he wouldn't be the man she'd been looking for, not by a long shot. But he was having such a great time that he wanted to put off the moment when he'd have to tell her, at least for a little while.

The house was dark except for the soft glow of the porch light. A sled was propped near the door, and crude drawings of Santa and Frosty the Snowman were taped to the windows. Russ started to set the two gifts on the rubber welcome mat in front of the door when the lock twisted and the door opened a crack.

"Is that you, Santa?" whispered a child from inside.

"Benny?" Russ asked.

"Yeah, Santa, it's me, Benny."

"Benny, I'm—"

"I've been real good, Santa. Want some milk and cookies?"

"I don't really—"

"They're right here, on the table. I thought you'd come down the chimney."

Russ thought of explaining who he was, but that would burst this little kid's bubble, and the quivering excitement in Benny's words was hard to resist. He deliberately deepened his voice. "Tell you what, Benny. I'll come in for a minute, and bring you your presents, but we won't turn on any lights and wake up your daddy, okay?"

"Okay," Benny whispered. He opened the door. In the glow from the porch light the boy stood there in his *Star Wars* pajamas and looked up at Russ in wonder. "Where's your red suit?"

"Sometimes I like to dress like a cowboy." Russ pulled his Stetson down over his eyes, hoping Benny wouldn't recognize him if he saw him some other time, like out at the ranch. Then he walked into the darkened living room, the packages under one arm.

"I like dressing like a cowboy, too."

"How come you're not asleep?"

"Kids *never* sleep on Christmas." Benny took Russ's hand and led him over to the fireplace. "The cookies are right over here."

Benny seemed more interested in feeding him cookies than finding out what was in the packages. Russ was impressed. He couldn't remember the last time he'd held a little boy's hand, and it stirred all sorts of warm, fuzzy feelings. "I'm real hungry, too," he said, still disguising his voice. "It's been a long night."

"I'll bet. I heard you coming. I saw your sleigh."

Russ wondered if he'd live to regret this idea. Benny would see the sleigh again one day when Steve started giving rides to tourists. Russ thought fast. "And you know what? I borrowed that sleigh from my helper, ol'

Steve Gibson, 'cause it fits in with my western clothes. I'm givin' it back to him after tonight."

"I know him! He let me ride his horse!"

"Better keep your voice down, son. Wouldn't want to disturb your daddy."

"Oh." Benny let go of his hand and picked up the plate of cookies. "Eat these, Santa," he whispered. "They're *good*."

Russ set down the packages next to the tree. "Want to have one with me?"

"I'm not s'posed to. They're for you."

Russ considered the three chocolate-chip cookies on the plate Benny held out. "Two's my limit, pardner. Mrs. Claus put me on a diet."

"But you're not fat. I thought you'd be fat."

"See how good the diet is workin'?"

"You could have three."

"Nope. Mrs. Claus wouldn't like it. You take one."

"Well…okay." Benny took the smallest cookie. After Russ claimed the other two, Benny put down the plate and picked up the glass of milk. "Here."

Russ figured the milk had been sitting there for maybe four or five hours at least. The parents were supposed to wait until the kids went to bed, then polish off the milk and cookies. Benny's dad hadn't done that. With all his worries, that was understandable. Maybe he planned to beat Benny out here in the morning, but with little kids that wasn't a very safe bet. He was beginning to remember what Christmas had been like when he was five, and he hadn't slept much, either.

He didn't dare tell Benny to drink the milk. If it was spoiled, Benny could get sick. Hoping that milk spoiled slower on a cold winter night, he took the glass. "Thanks." He gulped it down. It was terrible, but then he'd given up milk a long time ago in favor of beer. He probably wouldn't have liked it ice-cold, either. He took a big bite of cookie to kill the taste.

"Can I open my presents now?" Benny asked.

Russ swallowed a mouthful of cookie. "Don't you want to wait 'til mornin', when your daddy gets up?"

"Nope. He sleeps late."

Russ was kind of curious about the presents, himself. "Okay, let 'er rip."

Benny squatted and started in on the biggest package, which looked like a small hat box. Sure enough, there inside was the miniature Stetson that Steve used to wear when he was Benny's age. Russ had seen it hanging on a peg in their old bedroom for years. Steve must have decided not to save it any longer for the kid he might never have.

"Wow!" Benny took the hat out of the box as if handling a gold crown. "I never had one like this."

Russ tucked the second cookie in his pocket for Jo. Thinking about Steve giving up this hat was causing a lump in his throat that made it tough to eat, anyhow. He cleared away the hoarseness. "Let's see it on you, cowpoke."

Benny situated the hat on his head and glanced up at Russ. "How's that?"

"Let's tilt the brim a little more." Russ crouched and adjusted the hat. "There. That's perfect." In the darkness, it could have been Steve's boy, and Russ's eyes got kind of watery, knowing how much Steve had longed for the day he could pass on that hat.

Another kid's Stetson hung on the next peg in their old bedroom—the one Russ used to wear. Steve could use that hat if he needed one. Russ wouldn't need it. Damn, but all of a sudden he wanted to need it. And he knew who he wanted to help him make that kid, too. This Christmas stuff had him thinking crazy thoughts.

The hat still on his head, Benny squatted next to the box. "There's a letter in here."

Hot dog, Russ thought. Benny might need Russ to read the card to him. Then he'd know what Steve had been writing about to all these folks.

Benny peered at the envelope. "That's not how you spell my name," he said with some disappointment. "It must be for Daddy."

Russ was disappointed. He and Benny couldn't very well open a card addressed to someone else.

"Why did you send a letter to Daddy, Santa?"

"Uh, just wanted to wish him a merry Christmas."

"Oh." Benny dropped the letter back in the box and started on the second package. In no time he'd pulled out a hand-braided hatband. "Cool! I'm gonna look great!" He took off the hat and brought both the hat and hatband to Russ. "Can you help me put it on?"

"Sure." Sitting back on his heels, Russ took the hat and hatband. Even in the dim light he recognized Steve's work in the braiding. He'd gone to a lot of trouble to make a little boy happy, but Russ was beginning to understand the reward Steve got out of it. Once the hatband was snugged up around the crown, Russ settled the hat on Benny's head.

The kid's big grin seemed to light up the darkness.

"You look great, son," Russ said, his voice husky.

"Thanks, Santa. Did you like the cookies?"

"Outstanding." Russ adjusted the tilt of Benny's new hat again, not because it needed adjusting, but because he liked doing things for this kid. "Now, I'd best get going, and you'd best skedaddle off to bed."

"I'm gonna hang my hat on the bedpost."

"Yep, that's what cowboys do."

"I *know*." Benny started off toward his room. He turned back. "Merry Christmas, Santa."

"Merry Christmas, Benny." Russ watched him go down the hall. He couldn't remember a time when he'd had more regret for the way his life had turned out, and the stupid things he'd done. Benny might look up to him when he was parading around as Santa, but Russ didn't deserve that kind of respect as the hell-raising cowboy he really was, the man who had carelessly ended the life of someone else.

He rubbed a hand over his face and stood. With one last look around the room, he went out the door, locking it behind him. Benny's dad might have some troubles, what with his wife running off and all, but he had one terrific kid. Russ envied him that something fierce. Maybe next summer when he came back to work with Steve, he'd be able to spend time with Benny. With luck, the little boy wouldn't recognize him as the guy who'd pretended to be Santa Claus on Christmas Eve.

Jo HAD WATCHED Russ get caught at the front door of Benny's house. He'd stayed inside quite a while, although no lights went on in the house, so he must have been talking to Benny in the dark. She'd consulted the list and figured out the last stop on their route. She'd burrowed under the blankets as best she could, but she was beginning to shiver by the time he came back out.

His walk was slower than it had been going in, and she suspected he'd dealt with some emotional issues inside the bungalow. That wasn't all bad, she thought.

He pulled something out of his pocket before he stepped onto the running board and leaned toward her. "Have a cookie."

She smiled at him as she took it. "D—do you mean to tell me you've been in there eating cookies?"

He climbed in the sleigh. "And drinking the most godawful glass of milk in the world. You got cold waitin' for me, didn't you?"

"I'm f-fine."

"Just let me hold you a little while and get some of that chill off."

Jo moved into his arms gratefully. "Just don't forget we're parked in front of somebody's house."

"Not to mention Benny's nose is probably glued to the window right this minute." Russ wrapped his arms around her. "So I don't even dare kiss you. Eat your cookie. The sugar will give you energy and help raise your body temperature."

"I'd give anything for a hot cup of coffee to go with it."

"Soon." Russ tucked her head under his chin. "We're almost done."

Jo chewed a bite of cookie as she began to warm up within the security of Russ's embrace. "So Benny thought you really were Santa Claus?"

"Yep. He saw the sleigh from his window and heard the bells jingling. That's all it took."

"Was he surprised you weren't fat and jolly, with a white beard?"

"Maybe, but he wanted to believe so bad that he was ready to swallow any story I told him." His arms tightened around her. "And I do know what that's like."

She knew immediately what he was talking about. "Hey, cowboy, I'm telling you the truth this time. When we get back to my place, I'll prove it to you."

"And how're you gonna do that?"

"I'll let you go through my place with a fine-tooth

comb. I haven't had a chance to hide the evidence—if a guy lives there, even part-time, you'll know."

He paused, as if to consider that. "I reckon I would know, at that."

"Then, when you find nothing, your conscience will be clear."

"Oh, little darlin', my conscience probably won't ever be clear." He kissed the top of her head. "But that's not your concern."

She wondered if she dared ask. Finally she decided they'd shared enough that she had that right. "Don't be so sure. Talk to me, Russ."

He was silent for several seconds. "It's a long story."

"I'm a good listener." She waited, but he didn't go on. "It has something to do with Christmas, doesn't it?"

He went very still. After a moment he cleared his throat. "You warmed up enough to go to the last house on the list?"

"Russ—"

"Let's leave it for now, honey." He sounded as sad as she'd ever heard him. "I'll end up telling you the whole thing. I know that now. But let's leave it until later."

Jo's heart ached for him and she hugged him tight. "Okay, if that's what you want. But I know you much better than I did a month ago. You're a kind and gentle man, and you have strong principles. You couldn't possibly have done something that terrible."

He didn't respond as he released her and climbed out of the bed of the sleigh. "Where's the last present go?"

"To the Dutton family. The address was blurred, but I think it's on—"

"That's okay. I know where they live. Dave got himself stomped by a rodeo bull last year, and he's in a wheelchair, paralyzed from the waist down. Fran's holding things together for him and the two little girls."

"Oh, dear."

"He got hurt doin' what he loves, but still, it's rough on them. If I know Claire, she filled a basket from her supply of home-canned goodies in the cellar. She puts up the best wild-strawberry jam in the county. Those little girls go crazy for it."

"Then I guess we'd better make sure they have some for breakfast on Christmas morning."

"Guess so." Russ swung down from the running board and walked up to feed Blackie the last of the carrots from his pocket.

He hadn't leaned down to kiss her before he left this time, she thought. She hoped she hadn't pushed him away with her questions, but they needed to talk and settle a few things. The bond growing between them was too important to let secrets weaken it.

Colored Christmas lights winked from the porch roof of the Duttons' two-story house, and several blank spots showed that bulbs that had burned out hadn't been replaced. But what astounded Jo was that lights were on in every room of the house even though it was nearly three-thirty in the morning.

"Something's wrong," Russ said, pulling Blackie to a stop at the curb. "They wouldn't have all the lights on like that ordinarily."

"You're right." Jo tossed aside the blankets and pulled on her boot, although she didn't try to zip it over Russ's makeshift bandage. "That's why I'm going up there with you. They may need help."

Russ hopped down and picked up the last package on the seat of the sleigh. "You shouldn't be puttin' weight on your ankle. Stay put."

"Absolutely not. You can either help me out of here and let me hang on to you a little bit as we go up the walk, or I'll do it on my own."

"If there's somethin' really wrong in there, how can you help if you're stove up?"

"You never know. I could sit and talk to someone if they need comforting, for one thing. But if they need you to help, I'd rather sit inside for an hour than out in the sleigh."

"You've got a point there. I shouldn't have left you out there when I was talkin' to Benny."

"Oh, Russ, I didn't mean to make you feel guilty. I just—"

"Okay, here's how we're doin' this." He put the package on the running board. "You'll hold the present and I'll carry you."

"Oh, for heaven's sake. You don't have to carry me to the door. I'll feel like a fool."

"Them's my terms, sweetheart. Now just be quiet and cooperate. I can hear some kid screamin' in there."

"Yeah, me, too. All right."

"Just climb into my arms."

That wasn't such a bad assignment, she decided. She'd never known a man strong enough to hold her so effortlessly, but then she'd never known a blacksmith before.

"Now pick up the package and we'll be on our way," Russ said.

Jo grabbed the package and held it in her arms as Russ turned and started up the walk.

The closer they got to the front door, the louder the screaming. The pain-filled sound battered Jo's eardrums and made her wish they could turn around and drive away. The night had been filled with sweetness and laughter and joy, but that was obviously about to change.

"Put me down after we get up on the porch," Jo said. "They don't need to open the door and think they have another problem on their hands."

"I guess you're right. Just don't put your whole weight on that ankle. Lean on me as much as you have to."

"I'll be glad to, cowboy."

Russ walked up the wheelchair ramp instead of taking the steps, and then he set her gently down on the welcome mat. As she straightened her coat and fluffed the bow on the package, he rang the bell. He rang several times, and finally resorted to pounding on the storm door.

At last a girl about seven opened the door and stared up at them. She had on a flowered nightgown and bunny slippers, and her blond hair was tousled as if she'd recently been asleep. After looking at them in amazement, she turned and ran back into the living room. Shortly after that, a blond man in a wheelchair approached the door. His face was as white as the snow piled in a corner of the front porch. Jo figured he had to be Dave Dutton. When he saw Russ, he directed the little girl to open the door.

Once the door was open, the screaming became deafening.

"What's happened?" Russ asked, bending so that he could speak directly in Dave's ear.

Jo leaned toward them to hear the explanation.

"Marcy was sneakin' down to see if Santa had come, and she fell down the stairs in the dark," Dave said, his voice shaking. "I think her arm is broke."

"Has it been stabilized?" Jo asked.

"Yeah. Fran's had plenty of first aid," Dave said. "She took her in the kitchen, and I decided Kathy and I should just get out of her way. I think she's planning to drive Marcy to the emergency room, but she wasn't sure how to do that because the kid's hysterical, and I—" He gestured to his wheelchair. "I'm no help," he said, looking completely miserable. "We've been saving to get a modified car I can drive, but all we got now is my old truck, and Fran hates driving that thing, especially at night, and with the snow and all. It's got a balky clutch."

Jo's first thought, that she could take Fran and Marcy to the emergency room, died when she heard about the clutch. With her bum ankle, she wouldn't be safe driving a truck that was difficult even with two good ankles.

"I'll drive it," Russ said.

Dave looked at him. "But you don't drive."

Russ held his gaze, his expression grim. "Looks like I will tonight, buddy."

13

JO STOOD wondering what she could do to help as Russ headed toward the back of the house and the screaming child. The three of them left in the living room seemed to be held hostage by that terror-filled sound. Then gradually it grew a little less forceful, and finally settled down to soft whimpering. Jo shouldn't have been surprised. Russ had a way with frightened young creatures.

She let out a slow breath and glanced at Dave. The tightness around his eyes seemed to have relaxed.

"I'm Jo Cassidy," she said. "Russ didn't have time to introduce us."

Dave rolled his wheelchair toward her and held out his hand. "Dave Dutton. I don't know how you two happened to arrive in the middle of the night, but the angels must have sent you. Please, sit down. You must think we don't have any manners around here."

Jo eased down on the couch and unbuttoned her coat. "You're not supposed to worry about manners in a crisis."

The little girl who had let them in came over to stand in front of Jo. "Is that present for us?" she asked.

"Kathy, that's not polite," Dave said.

"Yes, it is for your family," Jo said, glancing down at the package in her arms. She'd forgotten she was holding it.

"Is it from Santa? Because there's a sleigh outside. I saw it when I opened the door."

Jo wasn't sure how to answer. "In a way it's from Santa," she said.

"In what way?"

"Katherine Marie," her father said, giving her a warning glance.

"Well, Daddy, I just want to know if it is or isn't. Because this kid at school said there wasn't any such thing as Santa. But I know you and Mommy didn't buy this present, so if it's really from Santa, then I can tell that kid to go jump in the lake."

Jo chuckled. What fun it would be to have a bright little girl of her own someday. "Then tell him to go jump in the lake, because this package is most definitely from Santa."

"Oh, *good*." She tilted her head to gaze at Jo. "How did you know it was a boy who told me there wasn't a Santa? I just said it was some kid."

"Was it a boy?"

"Yes. Kenny Longtree."

"Well, there you go. A boy told me the same thing once. You have to be careful about believing those boys."

Dave smiled, and it transformed his face from haggard to handsome. "I've been telling her the same thing," he said. "You can't trust those boys. Especially cowboys."

In the brilliance of his smile, Jo could see the dashing young man Dave must have been before the accident.

"Why's there a scarf wrapped around your leg?" Kathy asked. "It looks funny."

"I slipped on a patch of ice tonight and Russ made me an ice pack." Jo hoped that Dave would think the flush in her cheeks was from the cold. Thinking about the ice pack on her ankle reminded her of what had happened after that, and the memory made her tingle all over.

"We've got one of those gel things in the refrigerator," Dave said. "Once they leave for the hospital, we can get that and put it on your ankle."

"I'm fine," Jo said. It wasn't quite true. The ice pack had turned to water and her ankle was beginning to bother her again.

"We'll take a look, anyway. It's the least we can do," Dave said. "I—" He stopped speaking as a plump brunette came into the living room and his attention snapped immediately to her. "Where's Marcy?" he asked, his voice strained.

"Russ has her. It's amazing how he's settled her down. We're leaving for the hospital now. I just wanted to tell you." She glanced at Jo.

"Fran, this is Jo Cassidy," Dave said. "She arrived with Russ."

"Sorry to ruin your Christmas Eve like this," Fran said.

"Don't worry about—"

"Can I go to the hospital, Mommy?" Kathy interrupted, running over to her mother.

"No, honey," Fran said, giving her a hug. "You stay here with Daddy."

"Have you got the checkbook?" Dave asked.

"Yes, but we don't have much in—"

"Well, write one anyway. The banks won't be open until the twenty-sixth. We'll figure out a way to cover it."

"Okay, sweetie." She came over and kissed his cheek. "We'll be back soon. Be a good girl, Kathy."

"I'm *always* good," Kathy muttered.

Fran gave Jo another brief glance. "Nice to meet you. I wish it could have been under different circumstances." She gave Kathy another hug. "I'd better go."

"Good luck," Jo called after her, her heart aching for the little family. A hurt child and no money. Obviously, their insurance, if they even had any, wouldn't take care of this visit. She thought of Russ, driving for the first time in years, in a strange vehicle on icy roads. The sudden clutching at her heart finally made her admit how much he meant to her. She sent up a silent prayer that he would return safe and sound.

"Can we open the present now?" Kathy asked, returning to Jo's side.

"We're going to wait for Marcy and Mommy," Dave said. "They'll need a little Christmas when they get home, I expect."

He looked at Jo. "Let's see what we can do about that ankle. And something hot to drink. Coffee? In fact, I think there's a plate of Christmas cookies in the kitchen, right, Kathy?"

"Yeah!" Kathy said. "I helped make 'em, too. I know what, Daddy, let's pretend we're having a party. We could get out the cards and play Go Fish, and eat Christmas cookies, and play Christmas music on the stereo."

Trust a kid to organize the fun, Jo thought. "I think that's a great idea."

"I'll get the cards! They're upstairs!"

"Be careful on those stairs," Dave said, a note of fear in his voice.

"Okay." Kathy bounded up with no hesitation.

Dave shook his head. "She didn't even hear me."

"They never think something will happen to them."

"I didn't used to worry about it so much, either, until

last year." He sighed and looked down at the wheelchair. "Now I see disaster around every corner."

Suddenly being handicapped would be tough on anyone, but for an active rodeo cowboy, it might be worse, she thought. "You're probably entitled to a little paranoia. You got dealt a bad hand."

"Yeah, but it's a hell of a way to live. I spend most of my time now worrying about what could happen to the girls or Fran, and trying to think of ways to keep them safe. Then something like this happens anyway. I hate running scared. I've never been that way, and I don't like seeing it in myself."

Jo couldn't help thinking about Russ, who seemed to have a similar problem, although he had no obvious handicap like Dave's. Dave's sense of security had been destroyed by a stampeding bull, but she had yet to find out what had turned Russ's world upside down. "Do you know why Russ doesn't drive?"

"No," Dave said. "I figured he had to know how, because what guy grows up without learning these days? But when Steve takes him out on their horseshoeing jobs, Steve drives. When they go into town for a beer, Steve drives. Then when Russ heads back to Tucson to work at that dude ranch, he takes the bus. I asked Steve about it once, but he just changed the subject. When Russ showed up tonight, the first thing I thought was, great. I need somebody to handle the big old truck, and the good Lord sent me a guy who won't drive. But I guess Russ changed his mind about that."

"I guess he did." Jo wondered how much that decision was costing him right now.

ADRENALINE GOT Russ through the first half of the trip. Marcy wasn't screaming the way she had been, but she was crying softly, especially when the truck jostled her even a little bit.

Russ clenched his jaw and concentrated on making the drive as smooth as possible for the little girl who was probably dealing with the worst pain in her life.

But then the crisis was over and they had to come home. The break had been a simple one, and between the cast and a shot for pain, Marcy was doing fine.

Russ was not.

Too much was familiar about the scene. Here he was on Christmas Eve, driving down a snowy road with pine trees all around and a woman in the seat next to him. True, the vehicle was a clunky old pickup instead of a red Firebird, and there hadn't been a four-year-old involved on that night three years ago. But that didn't stop him from sweating so bad his hands were slick on the steering wheel.

In his mind, every dark patch in the road became a patch of black ice, and he could feel all over again the loss of control when they'd gone into the skid. His heart raced with every slip of the tire tread, and he kept hearing Sarah's scream as they'd flipped. It was the last sound he ever heard from the woman he'd loved, the woman he'd intended to marry, the woman who was supposed to be the mother of his children.

Get over it, he told himself now, but the images wouldn't go away. His chest grew tight as he struggled to breathe. The road was deserted, as it had been on that horrible Christmas Eve, and the truck's headlights glittered on a path that looked as if it was paved with broken glass. There had been a lot of broken glass that night. And the blood. Oh, God, the blood.... Russ began to shake so badly he couldn't hold on to the wheel.

Afraid he'd wreck them yet, he slowly brought the

truck over to the side of the road and managed to put on the brakes without sending them into a skid. Then he rested his head on the steering wheel and gulped in air as waves of nausea washed over him.

"Russ?" Fran sounded terrified.

"Sorry...I'll be...okay..."

She laid a hand on his shoulder. "Russ, you're sweating like you've been riding bulls. What is it?"

If he tried to explain, he might break down completely. He forced himself to take deep breaths. "I hate seeing...someone hurt." Well, that much was true. He hated seeing them dead even more.

"Bless your heart. You're having a delayed reaction to Marcy's accident, aren't you?"

"Guess so."

"Do you want me to drive? Marcy's almost asleep. You could hold her and I'll—"

"Nope." He filled his lungs again and lifted his head from the steering wheel. Then he tugged down the brim of his Stetson and faced the road—the devil that had almost beat him. He'd never realized what a damn coward he'd been, refusing to drive after that night. He might be a sinner, but he was no coward. "I'll get us home."

"I know some people react like you're doing," Fran said. "They get through a crisis just fine and fall apart afterward. Me, I just panic from the beginning."

"You did fine." He eased the truck back onto the slick road. His heart still beat fast, but the dizziness was gone. "Keep talking to me, Fran. It helps."

"Don't be ashamed of having a tender heart, Russ. You were wonderful with Marcy when you got to our house. I was as scared as she was, which wasn't helping."

"It's probably hard not to be scared when it's your kid."

"Oh, I have a feeling you'll still have that calm attitude even with your own kids, Russ." She chuckled. "And your wife can pick up the pieces after it's all over and you collapse."

A picture of Jo flashed through his mind. "I don't reckon that's very likely."

"What's not likely?"

"A wife and kids. I'm not the marrying kind."

"So you've said, but I find that hard to believe, Russ. From what I've seen, you'd make a wonderful father, and I suspect you'd be a darned good husband, too."

Although the conversation was helping him conquer his fear, he decided a different topic was in order. "How's work?"

"Frustrating. I've put in for a promotion, and I was hoping to get it before Christmas, but no such luck. We could really use the extra money, especially to get a car that's modified so Dave can drive it. He needs that, needs to get back to a more normal life. He's getting stir-crazy being so dependent on me."

Russ thought of how he'd hemmed himself in, not driving, and he understood the problem. "Fran, I've got some money put by, and I can't think what I'm ever goin' to do with it. I could—"

"Nothing doing."

"We could make it a loan, then."

"Russ, I didn't bring up the subject of my promotion just to make you feel sorry for us."

"I don't." Russ was surprised to realize that was true. Fran and Dave had each other and two wonderful children. "In fact, I'm kinda jealous of you, to tell the truth."

"Jealous?" Fran laughed softly. "That's rich."

"You may not have money, and Dave's in that chair, but you have a lot goin' for you."

Fran gazed at him for a long moment. "You know, you're right. You're absolutely right. I was forgetting that, and I appreciate the reminder. I haven't counted my blessings recently, and it's time I did."

"So you'll let me loan you the money?"

She laughed again. "What's that got to do with anything?"

"I've learned something tonight, delivering the gifts for Steve."

"I figured out that's what you were doing."

"Yeah, he and Claire took sick, so they asked me to help. And I found out why they've kept this up through the years. Passin' out these presents really makes a person feel...good."

"So loaning us the money would really be a favor to you?" Fran said softly, a smile in her voice.

"That's right. I don't take any pleasure gettin' my bank statement, but I sure would get pleasure thinkin' of Dave driving himself around, and knowin' I helped make that possible."

"Well, thank you, Santa. What a wonderful Christmas present. And look at that. You also got us home safe and sound."

Russ was startled to see that they were on the Duttons' street, heading for the driveway of the two-story house. Concentrating on Fran and her problems had pulled him through. It was something to keep in mind. "Can you get in the house okay without me?" he asked.

"Sure I can. But you should at least come in for a cup of coffee."

"Oh, I will, but I need to go see how Blackie's doing. He's been standin' in the cold for quite a while."

"See what I mean about you? That's the kind of thoughtful person who would make somebody a fantastic husband."

"Or a good zookeeper," Russ said with a grin.

Fran laughed. "Sometimes it amounts to the same thing, cowboy."

WHEN THE BEAM of headlights shone briefly through the living-room window as the truck swung into the driveway, Jo closed her eyes and muttered a little prayer of gratitude. She hadn't realized how tense she'd been, waiting for his return, but now she was giddy with relief. One look at Dave's face told her he was experiencing the same emotions.

"Well, do you or don't you?" Kathy demanded.

"Do I or don't I what?" Jo had completely lost track of what was going on.

"Have any *sevens*? I asked you twice." Kathy whooped with joy when Jo handed over her sevens. "I win! I win!"

"Time to quit, honey," Dave said. "Mommy's home."

"Finally." Kathy jumped up. "I'm going to see if Marcy has a cast on her arm."

"Hold it, kiddo." Dave blocked her exit with his wheelchair. "Give Mommy a chance to get in the door before you pounce on her. Marcy might be asleep."

"Oh, *Daddy*. I just—"

"Here we are," Fran said, walking in, holding a sleepy little towhead with a big cast on her forearm.

"Hi, Daddy," Marcy said. "I got a cast."

"Lucky ducky," Kathy muttered.

Dave held out his arms. "Come over here and let me see, Marcy-darcy."

"Did it hurt, Marcy?" Kathy asked.

"Yup," the little girl said. "They gived me a *shot*."

"Yuck." Kathy shuddered.

As Fran lowered Marcy into his arms and Kathy hovered nearby, Jo felt like an intruder on the intimate family scene.

She looked around for Russ, but he hadn't come in with Fran.

Getting up from the couch, she hobbled over to the window and peered out.

Russ stood on the curb, rubbing Blackie's muzzle.

Jo felt a rush of tenderness so strong she nearly walked right out the front door so she could be with him. She wanted to hold him and tell him what a wonderful thing he'd done, handling this crisis, and how much she... Jo paused. How much she what? Could the word that had come so quickly to her be the right one? It was a powerful word, and she wasn't in the habit of tossing it around.

She gazed at the cowboy outside talking to his horse, and the sweet ache in her heart was nearly unbearable. Lust had brought them together, no doubt about it, but lust was like the rhinestone earrings she liked to wear for fun—glittery and exciting, but not for every day. The emotion she was feeling now was more like the diamond earrings she'd coveted for years and never owned.

Maybe she was getting carried away by Christmas spirit, and didn't know her own mind tonight. But she'd felt the Christmas spirit many times before, and this was a heck of a lot more potent.

"He said he'd be in for coffee after he checked on the horse," Fran said, coming over beside her. "But you two don't have to stay if you don't want to."

"Oh, well, I—" Jo looked into Fran's eyes and saw understanding there. "It's up to Russ, really."

"I have a hunch he doesn't always know what's good for him, but I think he's beginning to find out."

"I hope so."

"Me, too." Fran followed Jo's gaze. "Look at him with that horse. He wants everybody to think he's just a no-good hell-raiser, but there's a lot more depth to him than that." She glanced at Jo. "Maybe he's finally found a woman who understands what's going on under the cocky tilt of that Stetson."

"Let's say I'm willing to try."

AN HOUR LATER, as she was tucked in the back of the sleigh and Russ was driving her home, Jo wondered how much effort it was going to take to pry information out of him. There hadn't been much time to talk while they drank coffee and watched the girls open the gift of wild-strawberry jam and homemade muffins.

But even now, when they were alone, Russ remained silent and apparently deep in thought. He'd carried her out to the sleigh and settled her in without a word, and definitely without a kiss.

"How was it, driving again?" she asked.

"Okay," he said without turning around.

"I'm glad you were able to do that."

"Yeah, me, too."

So much for finding out what was going on under his Stetson, Jo thought. Wrapping the blankets tighter around her, she gave up trying to have a conversation with him. Once they got to her house, they'd either talk or...they wouldn't. If Russ pulled the silent treatment and left, she'd have the rest of Christmas vacation to try to pull herself together before classes started again. She hoped it would be long enough.

When they stopped in front of her duplex, hers was the only window in the neighborhood with a light on. That wasn't surprising, she thought, considering it was nearly five in the morning.

As Russ climbed down and walked to the sleigh bed, she decided to give it the old college try. "If you unhitch Blackie, we can put him in the garage where he'll be warmer. My truck can sit out for a while."

Russ rested his folded arms on the sleigh as he gazed at her without smiling.

"We need to talk, Russ."

"I know."

She let out a breath. At least this time he wouldn't leave without a word.

"If you'll climb over here, I'll take you in first," he said. "Then if you'll give me your keys, I'll back out the truck and put Blackie in."

She followed his instructions. "I think I have a couple of apples in the house."

Russ gathered her into his arms. "That would be nice for him. He's put in a long night."

She snuggled against him, breathing in the spice and leather scent that she'd grown to cherish. Through his coat she could just barely feel the steady thump of his heart. "So have you."

He carried her up the walk. "I've put in longer."

"Russ, no matter what happens from here on out, I want you to know I've had the best Christmas Eve of my life."

"Me, too." It would have been the perfect time for him to pause, turn his face to hers and kiss her. Instead, he concentrated on navigating the steps up to her front door.

"You sound overjoyed about it."

He glanced at her then, and in the gleam from the porch light his gaze was melancholy. "Everything ends, Jo."

His tone of voice didn't reassure her. "What are you, the Ghost of Christmas Future? Hey, it's Christmas morning, cowboy. We delivered all the presents and made folks happy. Aren't you at all pleased about that?"

"Yeah, I am." He eased her to her feet. "And thanks. I couldn't have done it without you."

"You're welcome." She didn't care for his tone of voice. It was way too formal. She dug in her pocket for her keys and unlocked the door. Then she handed them to him. "While you're backing out the truck and putting the horse in, I'll find the apples for Blackie and maybe some eggnog for us. How's that?"

"That would be nice, Jo."

Dammit, she thought. He was already looking at her with regret in those brown eyes of his. He was preparing for the big parting scene. She could smell it, but doggone it, they'd come too far during this amazing night together to let it all end when the sun rose. What she needed was a miracle. Fortunately it was Christmas, and miracles seemed to hang around at this time of year. But just to be on the safe side, she'd try jump-starting the process.

14

RUSS HAD BACKED Jo's truck out and was leading Blackie into the garage when Jo came out the kitchen door with a couple of apples in her hand. She still wore her coat and boots, which was a good thing because the garage was only slightly warmer than outside. Blackie would appreciate even that much warmth, though, and Russ was grateful for the chance to put him inside.

"Will this spook him, being in here?" Jo asked.

"We can leave on the light, so he can see what's around him." Russ glanced at the walls of the garage and spotted some empty hooks on each side where somebody had once hung rakes and ladders. "I'll crosstie him to those hooks. He should be fine. No trouble for him to get into." Russ couldn't say the same for himself once he stepped inside the house with Jo.

She handed him the apples and a paring knife so he could cut the fruit into chunks for Blackie. The woman obviously knew her way around horses. He liked the way she stroked the gelding's nose and talked to him before she started back inside. He liked just about everything about Jo, to be honest, which was what made the next part so tough to think about.

"I'll go fix us that eggnog," she said on her way through the kitchen door.

"Okay." He sliced the apples and gave the pieces to Blackie, drawing out the job as long as possible. God, how he dreaded seeing the look on her face when she learned what kind of man she'd let herself care about.

And she cared about him. That cat was out of the bag. He'd seen the melting expression in her green eyes and heard the softness in her voice. She was dreaming about a home and little kids playing in the yard and pink roses growing by the front door, sure as the world. In a short time she wouldn't be dreaming about that anymore.

When he couldn't put off the moment any longer, he sighed and gave Blackie one last pat before opening the kitchen door. A bottle of rum sat on the counter, so this would be full-fledged eggnog she was offering him. Christmas music drifted in from the living room along with the scent of pine.

"I'm in here," she called.

There was a peg by the back door, and Russ just naturally found himself taking off his hat and hanging it there.

He unzipped his coat as he walked into the living room.

The Christmas tree was all lit up and pretty-looking, but it didn't match the glow Jo was giving off as she sat on the couch, two glasses of eggnog on the coffee table in front of her. She'd sprinkled nutmeg and cinnamon on top, just the way Claire did when she served eggnog at the Double G. The room was toasty warm, but for some reason Jo still had on her wool coat, although her feet were bare.

Remorse washed over him. She probably wasn't glowing. She probably had a fever. "You caught yourself a chill, didn't you? Now you're gonna be sick because the ride tonight was too cold for you, and I—"

"I'm fine, Russ." She smiled at him and patted the

couch next to where she sat. "Take off your coat and join me."

Totally confused, he took off his coat and laid it on the rocker before coming over to the couch. "Why don't you take off yours, then, if you're so fine? I still say you're sick and you don't want to tell me, just like you didn't want to admit to your ankle bein' sprained."

"I guess I'll have to take off this coat to prove to you that I'm not sick."

"Yep." He sat down next to her.

She picked up the glasses and handed one to him. "Well, first, let's drink a toast to spreading happiness on Christmas Eve. I think we did that, Russ."

"You're stallin' because you don't want me to find out you're sick."

"Humor me. A toast to happiness."

"Okay. Here's to happiness. Maybe the rum will do you good, at that." He touched his glass to hers.

"To happiness."

He looked into her eyes, bright with what was probably a fever well over a hundred degrees. Still and all, as they drank their toast he loved looking into those eyes. The eggnog tasted just right, creamy yet with that special jolt the rum gave it. "It's good," he said.

"Thanks. Christmas doesn't seem like Christmas without a little eggnog."

"And somebody to drink it with." The eggnog went down so easy he took another swallow. *Somebody special to drink it with*, he thought.

"Yes." She sipped her drink. "And I had no prospects of that until you showed up on my doorstep tonight. By the way, do you want to look around for evidence of a husband?"

"I don't need to." Some of the eggnog clung to her top

lip and he wanted so bad to lick it off. He took another swig of his own drink instead. Damn, but the rum tasted good after a long, cold night. Sitting here with Jo was just about the best treat he could imagine while still having his clothes on.

"I expected you to turn this place inside out looking for a safety razor or a chaw of tobacco."

"No point in wastin' the time. I believe you."

"Really?" She raised her eyebrows. "Why?"

"Just a feelin' I have." He didn't want to explain that it was a feeling of connection to her so strong, that if some other man stood in the way, he'd know. A man didn't stand between them, unfortunately. That would have been a whole lot easier to deal with.

He drained his glass. The rum had a very soothing effect, and he was grateful for some Dutch courage to help him confess his sins. But first he had to find out if she was all right. "Okay, enough stallin'. Take off the coat." He gave her a stern look. "And then when you start shiverin', I'll know you're burning up with a fever, just like I figured."

"Well, you're partly right." She put down her glass and slowly unbuttoned the coat. "I am burning, and I might start shivering, too. It's been known to happen."

He gulped. He'd been so sure she had on her long underwear and sweats under the coat that the skimpy red teddy she was wearing packed a bigger punch than it might have if he'd been expecting it.

"I didn't have time to shop for a present for you," she murmured, sliding her arms out of the coat. "So I decided to wrap up something I happened to have on hand."

"Ah, Jo." Predictable things began happening to him

as he gazed at her dynamite body barely covered by the red satin.

Her exotic scent reached out to him, teasing him with possibilities. He'd come into this house with such good intentions, too. No more kissing, and definitely no more making love. Just a conversation about the realities of life, and a quick goodbye.

Now here he was with rum warming his belly, Christmas carols playing and the most desirable, sweetest woman he'd ever known sitting next to him wearing a little scrap of soft material. "You don't play fair, sweetheart. We were supposed to talk."

She took his empty glass from his hand before winding her arms around his neck and leaning back to smile at him. "You can start unwrapping your present anytime."

The seductive pose made the most of her cleavage and a shambles of his willpower, but he tried one last time to be strong. "You probably ought to put that coat back on, Jo. We need to have a serious conversation."

"I was very hot under that coat."

"You'll get no argument from me on that. But we really shouldn't be...doin' this." His brain told him to get up from the couch while he still could, but his hands seemed to have a will of their own. They spanned her waist and lifted her onto his lap.

She was entirely too cooperative. She straddled his knees and slid forward, coming up against another part of him that definitely thought for itself and was quickly rising to the occasion.

"Is your ankle okay like this?" he asked. How he loved looking into her eyes, touching her face, just being close to her.

"My ankle is fine."

She was so beautiful, so perfect. Knowing that she wanted him was a miracle in itself, and he could tell she did. Her nipples were making the red satin poke out, and he couldn't stop looking at the impression they made on the shiny material. "Jo, I don't know if this is such a good idea."

"It's a very good idea." She wiggled against him. "We're good at this."

"That's the problem." She smelled so wonderful. He eased the strap off one smooth shoulder, all the while telling himself to stop touching her. "A fellow can't think straight when he's..."

He lost track of the conversation as he slid the other strap down. The top of the teddy, which wasn't very substantial to begin with, slipped off her breasts. He'd dreamed of this view every blessed night—Jo's breasts, all pink and plump, beckoning to him in the lamp's glow. Back in the sleigh the light hadn't been much good, but now...words from a Christmas poem ran through his mind—*visions of sugarplums*. The words sure seemed to apply in this case.

And then she did something that turned him into her willing slave. Sliding her hands up her rib cage, she cradled her breasts and lifted them in the most tantalizing invitation he'd ever seen. "Merry Christmas, cowboy."

With a groan he wrapped his arms tight around her, closed his eyes and buried his face against her breasts. Heaven. She was everything he'd ever wanted and more. He feasted like a crazy man, yet the more he had of her, the more he wanted.

She moaned in response and rocked gently against his straining erection. "I want you inside me," she whispered.

He ached to be there, too. But there was a problem,

one that he hadn't thought of when this episode started. He lifted his mouth from her breast and cupped her face in both hands. "Jo, stop. Stop, sweetheart. I don't have any—"

"But I do." She reached between the cushions of the couch, and like magic, a condom appeared in her hand.

He was so grateful that he didn't stop to question how the condom got there. She slid back enough to undo his belt and jeans. She was pretty fast, but he thought she'd never get done, and with every movement of her hands in that delicate area he lost another notch of his control. He was breathing louder than a freight train by the time she'd pulled down his briefs and put the condom on.

She'd taken the lead and he had to admit he loved it. As she rose to her knees and unsnapped the crotch of her teddy, he felt dizzy from wanting her.

Placing her hands on his shoulders, she looked into his eyes. "Remember this," she murmured.

When she straddled him, he cupped her bottom, but he let her set the pace. She took her time, sliding down over him with maddening slowness. Her gaze burned hotter than a forge, searing him forever. He wondered how he'd live, knowing he'd never have her look at him like that again.

At last he was in up to the hilt, and he clenched his jaw to keep himself from exploding. He wanted this to go on for a very long time, and he was used to being more in command of himself. Somewhere along the line she'd robbed him of that legendary control, and he was nearly helpless against the raging need inside him.

Her gaze continued to lock with his as she started her ride. Oh, he'd remember this, all right. He'd go to his grave remembering Jo as she looked right now, loving him with no holds barred.

She went easy at first, and he managed a small amount of restraint. But she got wilder, building the pressure with faster and faster strokes, until he lost all hope of holding back.

Yet he knew she hadn't made it over the edge herself. With a strangled cry of defeat, he clutched her bottom and exploded within her.

She rocked gently, absorbing his tremors.

"Jo," he gasped. "You didn't—"

"I will," she whispered. "Look at me, Russ."

He did, and it was glorious to see her eyes so full of light as she moved against him, increasing the friction as she came closer to her moment.

Her lips parted and her breathing became quick and shallow. "You...need to...know something," she said.

Ah, she was nearly there. For one brief moment he wondered if she'd tell him she was married, after all, and he didn't want to hear it, not now. He urged her on with a firm grip on her bottom. "Don't talk. Just feel."

"Russ..." She gasped and stiffened against him. "Oh, Russ...I love you!" The spasms took her then as she quaked in his arms. "I love you," she said again.

Pain knifed through his heart, although his body was warm, fulfilled, singing with joy. He'd let things go too far.

JO FIGURED she'd given it her best shot. If Russ could walk away after being reminded of what they had together, if he could turn his back on the love she'd proclaimed, the love she knew was burning inside him, as well, then he couldn't be saved from himself.

As she snuggled against him, he stroked her back and held her very tight. She waited for him to say that he loved her, too. It was pretty obvious that he did. Whatever problems they hadn't discussed would become un-important once he'd confessed what was in his heart.

"Jo, sweetheart, I'm not worth lovin'," he said at last.

It wasn't what she'd hoped to hear. She could argue with him and point out all the good qualities he'd dis-played recently, but that wouldn't get her very far and she knew it. "Why aren't you worth loving?" she asked, her cheek resting on his shoulder.

"Because the guy you've been lovin' so sweetly, the guy who's still buried deep inside you, is a murderer."

"No!" The denial came out of her before she realized it. She slowly eased back so that she could look into his face. It was not the face of a man who could kill another person. She would stake her own life on that. "No, Russ."

"I don't blame you for not wantin' it to be true. You don't want to think you've given your heart to such a man. I apologize for that, Jo. I should never have let my-self...I should have realized that we..." His troubled gaze searched hers.

"Would fall in love?" she finished for him. "Because that's what's happened."

"No." He shook his head and took her face in both hands. "You might think so now, but in a little while—"

"I love you." She let him have it full force, sending the message with her eyes as well as her words. "And you love me, whether you're willing to admit it or not."

He combed his fingers through her hair. "I can't let myself love you, Jo."

"You can't help yourself, cowboy." She wiggled against him. "We just proved that. And it's more than just physical attraction between us, too. You should see the way you look at me—take the way you looked at that Manx kitten and multiply it about ten times."

His gaze warmed as he stared deep into her eyes.

"Just like that," she said softly.

He took a deep breath and sighed. "I think this is a conversation we'd better have when we're both dressed. I'd count it as a big favor if you'd go put on some more clothes."

"I like the leverage I have right now."

His gaze was tortured. "Please, Jo. Please, darlin'."

"All right." She climbed off his lap. "But you'd better not disappear while I'm out of the room. I promise I'll hunt you down if you run off again like you did last time."

"I won't run off."

"Then I'll be right back." She put her arms through the straps of the teddy and eased off his lap. In her bedroom she pulled on the sweats she'd hastily discarded. By the time she returned to the living room, Russ had fastened his own clothing and was pacing the floor.

He turned as she came into the room. "Okay, let me get through this without any interruptin', okay? I've only told this story once, and that was hard enough."

"Could we sit down?"

"You can if you want. You should, and put that ankle up. I feel better on my feet."

She walked over to the couch and sat where he'd been positioned when they'd made love. The cushion was still warm. Following his instructions, she sat sideways and put both feet up on the couch. "I'm ready."

"I guess it started when my mom died of cancer five years ago. Then a year later Dad died, too. The doctors said it was pneumonia, but Steve and me think it was a broken heart. Anyhow, I always knew Steve would get the ranch and I'd get a hunk of cash, because Dad had explained it to us. That split was fine with me, because the woman I was engaged to had her whole family in Albuquerque and she didn't want to leave them."

Engaged. Jo's heart did a little nervous dance. He'd nearly married someone. He hadn't always been a restless loner.

"I hadn't expected Dad to die for a long, long time." He rubbed the back of his neck. "It was tough. I wasn't ready for it, and I sure as hell wasn't ready to inherit all that money." He glanced at her. "I blew a lot of it, takin' Sarah to Puerto Vallarta, buying a Thoroughbred Sarah fell in love with when we went to the races at Ruidoso. And I bought a bright red Firebird."

Jo could guess what came next and her heart ached for him. Any idiot could put the pieces together now, and she didn't want to watch Russ turn himself inside out. "I get the picture," she said, "and accidents happen, Russ. That doesn't make you a mur—"

"Let me finish." He had his back to her, but his tension was obvious from the rigid set of his shoulders. "We were supposed to spend that Christmas with her folks, but I wanted somethin' more romantic than a passel of relatives on Christmas Eve. She wasn't crazy about my idea, but finally she said we could rent a room at Cloudcroft for the night if I promised we'd be back for the big family dinner the next day. So we started off, and by the time we got up in the mountains it was snowin' to beat the band." He paused and heaved a sigh. "She wanted to go back."

"Oh, Russ."

"But I wanted that night alone with her. We had a fight about it, and during the fight I...stepped on the gas. I thought I was somethin', all right, in that fancy car. I was somethin', all right. We hit black ice." He shuddered. "I killed her."

Jo got to her feet and hobbled over to him. She looked into his eyes, dull with misery. "You didn't kill her! Not the way you're thinking, as if you meant it to happen."

"I meant to scare her," he said quietly. "I was mad because I thought she chose her folks all the time, instead of me. I told her she was a baby, tied to her mama's apron strings. I was feelin' mean and spiteful. It was more than an accident, Jo."

"Don't you think we all feel that way about people sometimes? Don't you think we all do stupid things because of it? Most of the time we're lucky and nobody gets hurt. You weren't lucky."

"Oh, I was damn lucky. Just a cut on my chest." He laughed bitterly. "The medics called it a miracle."

Jo gripped his arms. "It was a miracle, as far as I'm concerned. I will thank God every day of my life that you lived through that accident. I'm sorry about Sarah. I hate all that you've been through as a result. But you're here with me now, and we have a chance to make something wonderful out of that tragedy."

"Are you crazy?"

"Crazy about you."

He pulled away from her. "Think about it, Jo. Think about where this will all lead. Marriage, kids. How could I expect a kid to look up to me, want to be like me?" His tone became mocking. "Hey, son, if you're lucky, you can grow up to drive a fast car and kill the woman you love, just like your old man."

Jo put her hands on her hips, her chest tight with frustration. "Oh, I didn't realize only perfect men were allowed to be fathers. My mistake."

"I'm miles from being perfect, sweetheart." His gaze

pierced hers. "If I'd killed her with a gun, I'd be in prison, maybe for life. But I killed her with my carelessness and my damn pride. Her folks are totally messed up by this, and they hate my guts, which makes sense to me. The way I see it, my rights to a regular life died with her. I'd accepted that, but then I met you, and my thinkin' went haywire."

"It's called love, Russ."

He shook his head. "I have no business lovin' you or anybody."

"You can't help it. And you have every right to love me." She stepped closer. "Unless you're too much of a coward."

His head snapped back as if she'd slapped him. "And what's that supposed to mean?"

The words came spilling out, and she realized she was lecturing herself, too. What she was suggesting wouldn't be easy for either of them. "If you admit to loving me, you'll be fighting ghosts all the way. Getting engaged again, telling a woman you love her, planning a wedding—I'll bet all that pain you've stuffed down would come charging back."

"I haven't stuffed down anything."

"Ha. Then why don't you have a driver's license?"

His eyes took on a stubborn gleam. "Don't need one."

"Oh, yes, you do. If you marry me, you'll need one, because I won't chauffeur you around like Steve's been doing. You'll have to start *living* again, Russ. And someday you'll have to tell our kids what happened to Sarah. It's called being human instead of a god on a pedestal. My guess is that if you make it through all that, you'll be a far better father than somebody who's never put himself through that kind of hell."

He gazed at her, and for a moment there was a flicker of hope in his dark eyes.

She held her breath.

The flicker went out and he backed up a step. "You're blowin' this out of proportion, sweetheart. We had us some good times. I appreciate that. But I'd best be goin' now before we both say things we can't take back."

She stared at him. "You idiot."

"You're finally makin' some sense."

Rage washed over her. "You total, complete idiot! You're going to throw this away, aren't you?"

"You'll thank me for it someday, little darlin'." He walked past her and picked up his coat from the rocking chair.

"Russ, don't you dare leave me!"

"Blackie needs to go home," he said. "And so do I. I've overstayed my welcome, as it is. Take care of that ankle, sweetheart."

In disbelief she listened to him walk across the kitchen floor and go out the door. Moments later the garage door creaked. She kept expecting that he'd get outside and realize what a stupid mistake he was making. He'd remember the love they'd made, the love they could make in the years ahead. He'd come back.

But he didn't.

15

BLACKIE WAS a hell of a lot more eager to get home than Russ was. He had to keep a tight hold on the reins or the gelding would have tried to break a few speed limits on the way back to the Double G. Russ wanted time to think about what he was going to tell Steve and Claire about Jo's tagging along on the Christmas run.

He knew the story would be all over town in short order. Russ figured Steve might as well hear it from him, but he'd like a little breathing space to collect himself before making that revelation. There was a whisper of dawn in the eastern sky. Sick or not, Steve would be up soon. That boy hadn't stayed in bed a morning for the past twenty years.

Russ calculated how much time he had left before Steve walked out the back door toward the barn. He might just make it home, stable Blackie and escape to his little cabin before Steve showed his face. Considering that Russ had been delivering presents all night, he could legitimately sleep in as long as he wanted. That would postpone the discussion by a few more hours, at least.

Russ loosened his grip on the reins and gave Blackie his head. The harness bells jingled merrily as the considerably lighter sleigh skimmed over the snowy roads. Russ turned up his collar and pulled his hat down over his eyes as the cold wind whipped past. The chilly slap of the morning air felt good and smelled of freedom. For the time being, it blew Jo's claim that he was a coward right out of his mind. If only he and Blackie could keep going on like this forever, things would be just fine.

Blackie wasn't about to pass up the lane leading into the ranch. When the split-rail fence marking the edge of the ranch property appeared along the side of the main road, Blackie pricked up his ears and quickened his pace. He swung into the lane with such speed that the sleigh almost took out the rural mailbox beside the road.

"Whoa, boy!" Russ wrestled the horse for control of the homeward stretch. If he barreled into the clearing jingling and jangling like this, Steve would be out of bed in a shot. Blackie snorted his protest and strained in the harness, but he slowed down.

"Easy, boy," Russ crooned, keeping his grip firm. "Easy."

The lane curved and the two-story log ranch house came into view. No lights were on. So far so good. Russ had always loved coming around that bend and seeing the house with it's wraparound front porch and huge stone chimney, but this morning he had a knot in his stomach and a throbbing in his head that spoiled the usual pleasure of coming home.

Blackie swung right toward the red barn, the color just starting to show in the early-morning light. Steve and Claire had argued when it came time to repaint the barn last year, Russ remembered. Claire had wanted it to be brown, to blend with the rest of the buildings, but Steve had insisted it had to be red the way it had always been, the way every barn should be.

Russ had voted with Claire. He'd lost his taste for any-thing red. But Steve had talked Ned and Russ into help-ing him paint the barn while Claire was visiting her ailing mother in California. Russ had expected Claire to be fighting mad when she came home and found the red barn, but instead she'd hugged Steve and told him that if he needed the barn to be red that bad, it could be red.

Right after that, Steve bought the sleigh that Claire had always wanted, and the leftover barn paint had been just enough to put two coats on it. Russ had been impressed with the way Steve and Claire worked things out between them, especially after the endless fights he'd had with Sarah, where neither of them seemed to get what they wanted.

He'd been trying to keep Jo out of his mind the whole trip home, but as he pulled Blackie to a stop in front of the barn and climbed down to unhitch the gelding from the sleigh, there she was right back in his head. He couldn't seem to keep her away.

It was partly the good loving, but that wasn't all of it, maybe not even most of it. Jo warmed a special place in his heart. He kept thinking of how she'd cheerfully put up with all kinds of problems during their adventure. Sarah wouldn't have made it past the incident with the ladder and the cops. He could still hear Jo singing Christmas carols as they jingled down the road, and see the sympathy in her eyes when she figured out why Hector Barnes had become a hermit. Not very many women would have kept on with the journey after spraining an ankle, or would have agreed to make love in the back of a sleigh in the dead of winter. No doubt about it, Jo was one of a kind, just as Steve had said.

And that was exactly why he had to leave her alone, so she could find somebody better than him.

He worked quickly, and soon Blackie was snug and warm in the barn. Then Russ realized he couldn't feed Blackie without feeding the rest of the horses, or he'd have a mutiny on his hands. When he finished with that, he decided a note to Steve was in order, or Steve might feed the horses again when he came out. A note meant going into the ranch house instead of straight back to his cabin, but it couldn't be avoided. He'd be real quiet.

Walking through the back door into the kitchen, where he knew Steve would go first for a quick cup of coffee, Russ flicked on a light. He took a piece of paper from the pad Claire always kept handy for making grocery lists, grabbed a pencil from a cup on the counter and sat down at the long oak table. The coffee, on an automatic timer, was already perking, and boy, did it smell good.

The whole house smelled good, in fact. In spite of being sick, Claire had baked last night, judging from the pumpkin, apple and mince pies sitting on the counter. There were six pies, which seemed like too many for dinner, so maybe she was planning to freeze some for later. A slice was gone from a pumpkin, Claire's favorite, and an apple, Steve's favorite. The mince was for him.

The pine scent of the huge Christmas tree in the living room drifted in, along with the leftover aroma of the mesquite they must have burned in the fireplace last night. Russ pictured them cuddled on the big leather sofa, one of Claire's afghans tucked around them, while they shared pie and coffee and watched the fire.

They'd have put on some Christmas music, too, because Claire loved that, and they'd probably opened one special gift from each other, as they usually did on Christmas Eve. It was a wonderful picture, one he could never expect to see happening in his own life. The sudden feeling of unbearable loss paralyzed him, and he sat staring at the piece of paper, trying to remember what he'd meant to write on it.

"So you're home."

Russ glanced up, amazed he hadn't heard Steve's boots on the stairs. "Yeah, I'm home."

"How'd it go?" Steve walked over to the coffeemaker and took a mug out of the cupboard above it.

"We...I got everything delivered." Well, that should do it, he thought. Ol' Steve wouldn't miss a slip like that.

Steve didn't turn around or comment on the *we* part of Russ's answer, but that didn't mean anything. Steve could be a real cool customer sometimes. "Want some coffee?" Steve asked.

"I guess." He might as well have coffee to go with the lecture he was bound to get in a few minutes. He took off his hat and laid it on the table before slipping his arms out of his coat and hanging it over the back of the chair.

"How about some pie? Claire made a mince one in honor of you bein' here."

"I'll get it." Russ pushed away from the table.

"Hey, sit down. You've had a long night."

"Thanks." Russ wished Steve wouldn't be so nice to him. It made the story about Jo that much harder to tell.

"How're you and Claire feeling?"

Steve cut two pieces of pie and put each one on a plate. "I'll tell you about that after you fill me in on the trip." He took the time to warm the pie in the microwave. "Ice cream?"

"For cryin' out loud, Steve. You ain't no short-order cook. Give me the darn pie and somethin' to eat it with and I'll be a happy man."

Steve set the warm pie and coffee in front of Russ and grinned at him. "You should take the service when you can get it, cowpoke."

"You make me nervous, waitin' on me like that."

Steve sat down across from Russ and started in on his own piece of pie. "So tell me about it."

Russ enjoyed a bite of pie and a swallow of coffee before answering. "First off, those kittens nearly froze in that cage, so I put 'em under my jacket, and then one clawed me real good and I dropped the list in the snow."

Steve started to laugh.

"As if that wasn't bad enough, when I went up to Lucile Varnum's door with the kittens having a regular rodeo under my jacket, and I told her Santa Claus was paying her a visit, she thought I was drunk and wouldn't let me in."

Steve almost choked on his coffee. "I wish I coulda been there."

"You and me both. I was ready to punch you in the nose about then."

Steve looked at him, his gray eyes dancing. "So what'd you do then? Don't tell me the kittens are back in the barn."

"Nope. They're delivered." Russ thought how much Steve looked like their dad at that moment. Lord, but he missed the old man. He took another bite of pie. Now for the hard part. "I went next door and asked Jo to help me calm her neighbor down," he said.

Steve grew more alert. "Really? Did you meet the husband?"

"There ain't no husband, Steve."

Steve's eyes narrowed as he gazed at Russ. "What do you mean, no husband?"

"I mean, she made it all up. I think it had somethin' to do with keepin' her from making another mistake like that night she took me home. I guess she has a weakness for cowboys."

Steve stared at him. "I'll be damned. So you knocked on her door, and she answered and told you she wasn't married, just like that?"

"No, I thought she was married for most of the night. That's why I didn't—" Russ brought the story to a screeching halt as he realized what a mess he was making of it.

Steve seemed to have forgotten all about his pie and coffee. "Are you telling me that Jo went with you to all the houses?"

"Well, see, at first I thought she was a lonely woman with a no-account husband who'd left her to go chasin' around on Christmas. So I felt sorry for her, and she really wanted to go on the rounds."

"And later, when you found out she wasn't married, you stopped feeling sorry for her."

Russ tried to meet his gaze and failed. "You could say that."

"You slept with her again, didn't you?"

Russ shoved away the rest of his pie and coffee. "Look, I don't need you to tell me that was a mistake. That woman just gets to me. But it's all been taken care of."

"Is that right? How did you take care of it?"

"I told her about Sarah."

Steve leaned back in his chair and studied his brother. Finally he shook his head. "I'm sorry, but you'd best spell it out for me, Russ. I don't figure how telling her about Sarah takes care of anything."

"It's plain as day. A woman like her doesn't belong with a man like me. She'll see that when she has time to think about it."

Steve frowned. "But she didn't run away screaming once she found out about Sarah, did she?"

"Not exactly, but once she thinks about it, she'll know I'm not the kind of guy she—"

"Russ, is that woman crying her eyes out because you've left her again?"

"Cussing me out is more like it. She was pretty mad when I left. Called me an idiot."

"That makes two of us who hold that opinion."

Russ got up from the table. "You're not thinkin' straight, either. Supposin' that Dad had come to us one day and said, 'Boys, you need to know somethin'. I drove careless one night and killed the woman I was going to marry.' Would you have looked up to him after that?"

Steve considered the question. "Yes, I would."

"You're just sayin' that because you want to make a point."

Steve got to his feet, too. "I'm *sayin'* it because it's the truth! Dad would've picked a time when we were old enough to understand. And by that time I'd know what kind of man he was! I wouldn't judge him for a mistake in his past."

"You're just talkin' through your hat! I say you'd wonder how a guy could kill his fiancée and then just go on and marry somebody else, calm as you please, like that woman he killed meant *nothing* to him."

"You don't want to hear the truth, do you? Well, I'm gonna give it to you anyway!" Steve pointed a finger at him. "You didn't really love Sarah."

Anger boiled hot in Russ's belly. "The hell I didn't!"

"You think all this grievin' will make up for it, but you didn't love her, cowboy. I knew that the first time you brought her home. You kept tryin' to make it right with her, but it never was. She was a spoiled brat. And *that's*

the burr under your saddle, because you found somebody you can love. And you don't want to own up to
that, because then you'll also have to own up to the truth
about Sarah!"

Russ gripped the back of the chair to keep himself
from lunging across the table. He stood there breathing
hard and glaring at Steve. "You are so full of it, brother.
I can't believe—"

"Merry Christmas, boys."

Russ closed his eyes at the sound of the soft voice so
like his mother's. Their fight had gotten Claire out of
bed. She'd baked pies and decorated the house and knit
afghans to welcome in this special time of year, and now
her husband and brother-in-law were paying her back
by shouting at each other on Christmas morning.

He turned. "I'm sorry, Claire. Really sorry." He
grabbed his coat and hat and bolted for the door.

"Russ!" she called. "Don't—"

"Let him go," Steve said. "If he's set on makin' a
damn fool of himself, I reckon there's nothing we can do
to stop him."

She'd really done a number on herself, Jo thought,
hobbling back and forth in the small living room. She
couldn't even pace decently and wear off some of her
fury. Damn Russ. And damn herself even more, for
thinking there was enough magic in Christmas to give
her a happily-ever-after. She'd dreaded being alone this
morning, and thanks to her own stupidity she was *really*
alone.

Exhausted as she was, she doubted she'd be able to
sleep. Presents from her parents waited under the tree,
but she wasn't in the mood to appreciate them. Then she
remembered the tape her mother had sent her of *It's a*

Wonderful Life. For the first time she could remember, she hadn't watched the movie on Christmas Eve, and in spite of everything, she hated to break the tradition.

"Actually, it's a crummy life," she muttered, but lacking any better plan, she turned on her television, started the VCR and plopped onto the couch. Then she remembered what had happened there and moved to the rocker. Maybe tomorrow she'd put an ad in the paper and sell the couch. Better to sit on the floor than be reminded of that no-good Russ Gibson, the man she wished to hell she didn't love.

At first she didn't pay much attention to the movie, which she knew by heart anyway. Instead, she kept replaying everything that had happened in the past few hours and cursing herself for being six kinds of a fool. Previous experience told her that eventually her anger would let up, and she wasn't looking forward to the misery that would follow. Right now she wanted a dartboard with Russ's face on it, but thunder and lightning meant rain was sure to follow. Lots of rain.

Gradually the movie drew her in, and she found comfort in the familiar scenes, almost as if her parents were sitting with her. Yes, watching the movie had been the right thing to do. It reminded her of who she was, and what she stood for. If Russ was too stupid to value that, then she was well rid of him. Of course she was.

Something about the Jimmy Stewart character engrossed her more than usual, and finally she understood what it was. His guilt and feelings of worthlessness reminded her of Russ. With that insight, the anger ebbed a little and the first tears began. She watched the movie through streaming eyes as she cried for herself, but also for Russ, who had no angel like Clarence to show him what an idiot he was. Russ's story would make a lousy movie.

She had to pause the picture to hobble into the bathroom for a box of tissues, and by the end of the movie she'd created a mound of used ones on the floor. Pale sunlight peeked through the windows as the final credits rolled. With a sigh, Jo got up to shut off the television. What a merry Christmas this was shaping up to be.

When the phone rang, she told herself it wouldn't be Russ. Her parents, most likely, and she hadn't even opened their presents yet. As she walked into the kitchen to answer it, she planned her response. She'd say she'd slept in and would call them back once she'd opened everything.

The male voice on the other end of the line didn't belong to her father. "Jo?"

Her heart slammed against her rib cage until the caller identified himself.

"This is Steve."

"Oh." Her breath came out in a whoosh. "Steve."

"You figured it was Russ, didn't you? I'm sorry. We sound alike on the phone."

"It's okay. I don't want to talk to him, anyway."

"I'm sure you don't. I'm not real fond of that ol' boy myself right now."

"So he told you about last night?"

"Enough. Then we sort of...got into it, and he took off."

The hollow place inside her felt big as a barrel.

"He went back to Tucson?"

"Nope. He might've considered it, but the roads are still pretty bad and a new storm is supposed to come in this afternoon, so the bus schedule is all screwed up. He saddled up his bay and rode out, probably headed for the lake or someplace like that."

"Is he...is he okay?"

"Physically. He said he told you about Sarah."

"Yes." Funny, Jo thought, that a woman had come between her and Tommy, and it was happening again with Russ. Only this time the woman was dead.

"How do you feel about that?"

"I told him exactly how I felt about it. He made a mistake, a really bad one, but we all do stuff like that. Most of the time we don't get caught. He did, but that doesn't make him any worse than the rest of us, just more unlucky."

Steve heaved a sigh. "Jo, I've talked this over with Claire. We've been talkin' and discussin' for a couple of hours, and Claire's finally convinced me to try one last thing. We'd like you to come along with the other folks who're invited to Christmas dinner today. If you'll do it, I'll pick you up when I come to fetch Lucile about three this afternoon."

"Lucile?" Jo frowned. "You invited her to dinner?"

"We invited everybody on the list."

"But I thought you and Claire were sick? Should you be—"

"We weren't sick, Jo. Before we picked Russ up at the bus stop, we ate a pile of Claire's homemade horseradish sauce, and that'll make your nose run like crazy. I guess we were pretty convincin'."

Jo leaned against the counter as she began to feel lightheaded. "Wait a minute. Are you telling me you staged this whole thing to force Russ to make your rounds for you?"

"You got it. Recently, he's spent Christmas Eve with a bottle, focusin' on his misery, which ain't getting him anywhere. Claire and me, we know what an upper playing Santa is, and we figured it might be enough to cancel out his bad memories. We just didn't count on you goin' along."

"Oh my God." Jo put a hand to her tight chest. "I ruined it for you, didn't I? Now he's in worse shape than ever."

"I wouldn't say that, Jo." Steve cleared his throat. "Matter of fact, I'd say my little brother's head over heels in love."

16

JO PILED OUT of the ranch van that afternoon along with the happy crowd of people she'd met individually the night before. She'd found out that the card in each present had explained that Steve and Claire had faked their illness to nudge Russ into the Christmas spirit, and they'd be perfectly well to host a big celebration dinner today. Everyone on the list was invited and Steve would come by for them in the van. No wonder everyone had been so secretive about their message inside the card, Jo thought.

"Does Russ know yet that this bunch is coming for dinner?" she asked Steve as they all trooped to the front porch.

"I was gonna tell him. I'd planned to come clean about pretendin' to be sick, too, but once we started shoutin' at each other, I just let it go."

"Is he here?" Jo glanced around the snowy landscape, expecting to see Russ out by the barn or over near the corrals.

"Haven't seen him since he rode out this mornin'."

Jo pulled her coat tight against the wind and glanced up at the clouds. "He'd better get home soon. They've predicted another bad storm."

"He was born in these parts. He oughta know how to read the weather by now." Steve turned to Ned as the little crowd reached the wide steps leading to the porch.

"We don't have no ramp for Dave's chair, so you and me are gonna lift him right up these steps, chair and all."

"That'll be *fun*, Daddy!" Kathy said. "Just like a ride at the fair, right, Benny?" She'd immediately made friends with the little boy who wore his spiffy new cowboy hat so proudly.

Benny tugged the brim of his hat over his eyes, obviously copying a move he'd seen adults use. "Right."

Jo smiled. She'd met Benny and his father, Matt, for the first time today, and she'd done her best to act amazed as Benny had told her about Santa's visit during the night.

"I wanna sit on Daddy's lap," Marcy said.

Ned laughed and picked her up. "Why not? Anybody else want to hitch a ride? Steve and me can handle it."

"Hey," Dave said, grinning at him. "Stop showin' off your danged muscles for your bride and get me up there. I'm powerful hungry, and I can smell the turkey from here."

While Steve and Ned carried Dave and Marcy up the steps with Kathy and Benny hopping along beside them, Jo looked around to see if Lucile needed help. Apparently not. Hector Barnes already had her firmly by the arm and was escorting her up to the porch.

"I saw that movie," he said to Jo as he passed her. "Not bad."

"Glad you liked it." Jo had half expected Hector to bring his teddy bear to dinner, but he'd come out of his house alone. Under his heavy winter coat she'd glimpsed a red plaid bow tie clipped to the collar of his shirt. He and Lucile had ended up sitting together in the van. Although Lucile had done most of the talking, telling Hector about the kittens she'd closed in the bathroom while she was out visiting, Hector had seemed happy to listen.

Dave's wife, Fran, paused at the foot of the steps and turned to Jo. "By the way, did Russ tell you what he offered to Dave and me?"

"No, he didn't."

Fran looked like a different woman this afternoon. Her brown hair was curled into a soft style and she wore makeup, but the sparkle in her eyes would have made the makeup unnecessary. "Dave is so eager to thank him. Russ is loaning us the money to buy a car with hand controls so Dave can drive again."

"That's wonderful." Jo's heart ached at this new evidence of Russ's goodness. Yet he was unwilling to give himself any credit.

"You're telling *me* it's wonderful. Dave spent the day talking to me about what kind to get, and we've decided on something that would be good for traveling, so one day we can take the girls to Disneyland. I haven't seen Dave so excited about anything since before the accident. It's like a miracle."

"Be sure and tell Russ that when you see him," Jo said.

"I will. I guess he must be inside helping Claire."

"Not yet. But I'm sure he will be soon." Jo glanced up at the clouds as a snowflake gave her cheek a damp kiss. *Get home, cowboy,* she whispered to herself.

She had the urge to wait on the porch so she'd be the first one to see him when he rode in, but if he saw her, he might just ride back out again. She started up the steps alongside Elaine and her baby, who was fast asleep in a baby carrier that doubled as a car seat. The new afghan was tucked up around Amanda's chin, and she had her fist curled around the edge of it.

"I guess the blanket's working," Jo said.

"Like a charm." Elaine smiled at her. "My theory is that Claire made it with such love that she crocheted good feelings right into the pattern. Amanda can feel all those good vibrations. She's been a little angel ever since you and Russ arrived last night."

Jo smiled down at the sleeping baby. "Well, it's Christmas, after all. That's when angels show up, isn't it?"

"Like you and Russ, for example. This Christmas has turned out to be a much better one than I thought it was going to be. I called my parents this morning."

Jo gave her a quick glance. "Really?"

"I told them the whole story. Took Russ's advice, after all, and spilled the beans. They were great. They want me to come home to Texas so they can watch Amanda while I find a job there and get back on my feet. I've decided to accept their help."

"Good for you." Jo put an arm around the woman and gave her a hug.

"Is Russ inside?"

"Not yet," Jo said again.

"He's my backup in case Amanda turns fussy," Elaine said. "Look at that wreath on the door, Jo. Big as a truck tire. Claire and Steve really know how to make Christmas special."

"Yes, they sure do." Jo turned around before going in the door and scanned the treeline. Nothing. Her stomach clutched as snow started falling steadily and the wind picked up, swirling it over the empty yard.

Steve was right, she told herself. Russ was too savvy a cowboy to let himself get caught in a snowstorm. He'd consider his horse even if he didn't care about himself.

Hoping that her conclusions were right, she walked into the house.

The scene inside made her gasp with pleasure. A fire blazed in the huge fireplace made of smooth river rock, and a pine garland decorated with bandanna bows looped along the edge of the oak mantel. Hector, Lucile and Matt stood in front of the fireplace sipping from mugs and talking. The three older children sat in front of the tree playing with a wooden train set. The tree itself, which had to be at least twelve feet tall, was covered with western ornaments of every description—miniature saddles, boots, hats, spurs and lariats, all interspersed with chili-pepper lights.

The rest of the guests were seated on the rustic leather furniture grouped around the fireplace. Afghans in red and green lay over the arms of the sofa and chairs if anyone got chilly. For added color, poinsettias were scattered around the room, along with bowls of red and green apples. The mingled scents of roasting turkey, sweet-potato casserole and steamed winter squash reminded Jo that she'd had very little to eat all day.

A petite woman with curly black hair came toward Jo with a smile and a cup of steaming liquid. "Have some hot apple cider," she said. "I'm Claire. And you have to be Jo, because you're the only woman in the room I've never met."

"It's good to meet you." Jo took the mug of hot cider and glanced into Claire's friendly blue eyes. "Thanks. My mother used to make this back home."

"You must miss being home for the holidays."

"I do." Jo sipped the cider, which tasted exactly like her mother's. "But this sure helps. I felt so welcomed when I walked in here just now. I can't believe I haven't met you before, but you've never come into the Roundup with Steve, have you?"

Claire laughed. "Steve and I spend lots of time together at the ranch, and I figure he needs one little hidey-hole that belongs to him alone." She gazed at Jo and her smile faded. "Thank you for coming today. This can't be easy for you, considering the way Russ has been acting."

"No, it wasn't easy." Jo took a steadying breath.

"But I keep thinking about Clarence."

"Clarence?" Jo looked puzzled.

"The angel who saves Jimmy Stewart in *It's a Wonderful Life.*"

"Oh, *that* Clarence. The angel who keeps him from committing suicide by showing him how much good he's done for others."

Jo nodded. "That's the one. I love that movie."

"Me, too. We could use a Clarence today. Are you volunteering?"

Jo grinned. "I can't claim to be an angel, Claire."

"Oh, I don't know about that." She squeezed Jo's arm. "If that rascal of a brother-in-law would just show up, we could find out."

"I don't like the looks of this weather."

"He'll be in any minute," Claire said with determined cheer.

"Sure. Any minute." The wind howled down the chimney, causing the flames to dance wildly.

Claire glanced out the window and over at her husband, who was sitting next to Dave's wheelchair and having an animated discussion. "If Steve's not worried, I won't be worried." She looked back at Jo. "Russ will have a big appetite after such a long ride. I'd better check on things in the kitchen."

"Could you use some help?"

"Sure. Let's think positive and assume that we'll need to learn how to operate in the same kitchen one of these days."

Jo choked on her cider.

"Easy, sweetie." Claire patted her on the back. "That is what you're going for, isn't it—marriage, family, the works?"

Jo wiped her eyes, cleared her throat and looked straight at Claire. "Damn right I am."

"That's my girl."

JO HAD CALLED HIM an idiot, and he was proving it, Russ thought as he pulled his bandanna up over his nose and mouth and tugged his hat farther down over his eyes. Ears pinned back, his big bay moved steadily through the swirling snow, and Russ gave him his head, knowing the horse had more sense than the rider, and was more likely to find his way home. If they were going in the right direction, the huge rock Russ used to climb as a kid would show up on his left.

It would serve him right if he froze to death out here. He'd probably make things a lot easier on everybody else, too, if he just let nature take its course. But his horse didn't deserve that, and so he'd stick with him and make sure he got back to the barn.

God, it was cold out here. To keep his mind off the frigid weather, he thought about Jo. Nobody would have to know of his private imaginings and accuse him of loving her, after all. Just remembering the warmth of her arms and the light in her eyes when he'd made love to her was enough to make him not mind the stinging of the snow in his eyes and the bone-chilling temperature.

Jo. She'd been right about the driver's-license thing.

Driving Dave and Fran's truck over the icy streets had proved to him that he could handle the stress, and he couldn't depend on other folks to get him around anymore. With a license, he could buy a truck and a horse trailer and take his big bay, High Noon, to Tucson instead of leaving him in Prescott to get barn sour during the winter.

A sober night with Jo had also convinced him to give up the booze each Christmas Eve and come back to the Double G so he could help Steve and Claire with the deliveries. They'd invited him before and he'd always turned them down, figuring a no-account cowboy like him shouldn't be parading around as Santa Claus. Then he'd discovered nobody cared if he was a saint or not. They just liked the excitement of a Christmas Eve visit, and come to mention it, so did he.

He kept watch for the rock, but he'd lost track of time. The snow could do that to you. He pictured Jo ahead of him, urging him forward with that wonderful smile. He loved seeing her smile. There. Was that the rock or had he imagined it? The snow was so thick he couldn't tell for sure. Yeah, it was the rock. His sorry hide was saved, but more important, his horse wouldn't die out here.

Beyond the rock was the clearing where his mom and dad had built the Double G, using money his dad's aunt had left him. Russ could barely make out the house and barn, but his horse knew right where he was going. Russ leaned down and patted his neck. "Good job, High Noon. Oats for you once we get inside that barn."

Getting the barn door open with the wind blowing was a trick, but Russ finally managed it. He rubbed High Noon down real good and gave him his treat. Then he wrestled the door open and shut it again before plowing his way toward the house. He would have preferred to go straight to his cabin for the rest of the day, but he had one other job to do. He had to apologize to Steve and Claire for getting their Christmas off to a bad start.

He pictured them inside having an intimate little Christmas dinner. They'd probably want to bring up the subject of Jo, but he wouldn't let them talk about her anymore. Steve sure had some crackpot ideas, saying Russ hadn't loved Sarah. He'd planned to marry her, hadn't he? Of course he'd loved her. Jo wasn't anything like Sarah, and he wasn't in love with Jo because he didn't want to be in love with her or anyone.

If he'd fallen in love with Jo, he'd want to marry her, and he didn't want to marry anyone, either. What a disaster, living every day with someone who knew the worst about you. Living with Jo would be a nightmare. Sure, they'd have a great time in bed, and she was easy to talk to and laugh with, but now that she knew about him, her feelings would change. He could bet on it.

He went in the back door because he was covered with snow and the kitchen was the best place to take off his jacket and hat. He opened the door and stepped inside. Then he stared in speechless amazement at the two women standing there.

Jo and Claire whirled at the same moment.

"Thank God!" Jo cried.

The welcoming light was in her eyes, just the way he'd imagined it when he was fighting his way through the storm.

She looked so damn good that he wanted to walk over and take her in his arms. He even found himself starting in that direction, before he woke up and realized that would be another mistake in a whole line of them. He found his voice, although it sounded a bit rusty. "What are you doin' here, Jo?"

"Steve and I invited her," Claire said, lifting her chin. "And you will be civil, Russ Gibson, or I'll—"

"Claire, did I hear Russ?" Steve bolted through the kitchen door and paused, his anxious expression hardening as he looked at his brother. "Well, look what the cat dragged in. Is your horse okay?"

"He's fine." Russ gradually realized that the noise he was hearing from the living room wasn't the sound of the television set. "Who else is here?"

"Everybody you took presents to last night," Steve said.

Russ looked from his brother to Claire, a suspicion growing in his head. He remembered the extra pies on the counter this morning. "You've had this planned a while, haven't you?"

"Yes," Claire said. "But—"

"How did you know you'd be well enough, considerin' how sick you were yesterday?"

Steve and Claire looked at each other, guilt all over their faces.

"You faked bein' sick, didn't you?" The heat of anger chased away the chill in his bones. "You knew I'd have to go on that run if you pretended to be sick." He swung a hand toward Jo. "Was she part of the plot, too? You probably knew she wasn't really married all along, didn't you? Figured you'd play a little trick on me."

Jo started toward him. "They didn't plan that. Nobody knew I wasn't married except Lucile. That part was an accident."

He backed toward the door. "I don't know why I should believe you. I don't know why I should believe any of you."

"Dammit, Russ, you didn't give us any choice!" Steve bellowed. "All we're tryin' to do is make you see that—"

"That my family lies to me?"

"Straight talk wasn't workin' worth a damn!"

"Well, this ain't gonna work, either." Russ jammed his hat tighter on his head and went back into the snowstorm. *Tricked*. The whole thing had been a plot to get him hooked into Christmas. He wondered how much Jo had been a part of it. He felt sick inside at the thought that she'd known all along he was being played for a fool. Not that it mattered whether she'd been in on the plot. She was nothing to him. Nothing at all.

CLAIRE TURNED to Steve. "That sure turned out well."

Jo stared at the kitchen door, her heart thumping wildly. "It might yet," she said. "He won't leave, will he?"

"Nobody's goin' anywhere until this snow lets up," Steve said. "I imagine he's headed for his little cabin to nurse his wounds."

"He doesn't stay here in the house?" Jo asked.

"No," Claire said. "There's a little guest cabin out beyond the corrals. Steve's mom was a painter and she used it for her studio. Now Russ stays there whenever he's in town. I think he likes the reminder of his mother. He loved her very much."

Jo took a deep breath. Her plan might not work, but she was willing to try based on one thing—the look in Russ's eyes when he'd first walked in the door and seen her there. She'd waited a lifetime for that look. She wasn't giving up the chance to see it again without a fight.

"Okay," she said, glancing at Steve and Claire. "Here's my idea."

BECAUSE EVERYBODY ELSE raved about the meal, Jo was certain it was delicious, but she couldn't taste a thing. She ate to avoid insulting Claire's cooking, but she might as well have been chewing on Styrofoam packing peanuts. She kept glancing out the window at the swirling snow and imagining that it wasn't as thick as before. Her plan wouldn't be as easy if the blizzard continued full force.

The eating seemed to go on forever, which made everybody happy except Jo, and perhaps Steve and Claire. She could tell they weren't completely focused on the celebration, either. Finally, after Ned's third helping of pie, it looked as if everyone had filled themselves at the Gibsons' hearty table.

"Let us clean up," Fran said. "We've made enough mess to give you serious dishpan hands, Claire."

"Uh, if you'll all bear with us," Steve said, standing at the head of the table, "we have a bigger favor to ask than doin' dishes."

"Now, Steve," Ned said with a chuckle. "Are you plannin' to have us muck out your stalls? 'Cause I ain't dressed for it."

Steve grinned. "Maybe later. I can give you a change of clothes. But that's not what I'm talkin' about right now. All of you had a visitor last night."

"Santa Claus!" Benny said, jumping out of his chair. "He said he knew you!"

Uh-oh, Jo thought. Benny could be a problem. Well, Russ would just have to bluff his way through it.

"Yeah, where's Russ?" Dave asked. "I thought I heard him come in the back, but then he didn't show up for dinner. I wanted to talk to him."

"That's what I wish all of you would do," Steve said. He glanced out the window. "The snow's lettin' up a little, and I can drive us over to his cabin in the van. Russ doesn't seem to think he...has much to celebrate this Christmas."

"What a shame," Lucile said. "He made my holiday with those kittens."

"And that baby blanket was a lifesaver," Elaine said. "I know you made it, Claire, and I thank you. But when Russ and Jo arrived, my whole Christmas started to happen. I'd like a chance to tell him."

"Me, too," said Hector Barnes.

Benny gazed around the table. "What's everybody talking about? Didn't Santa come to your houses?"

"Yes, he did, Benny," Fran said. "And Russ brought him."

Jo sighed with relief. Keeping the faith in Santa obviously required the touch of an experienced mother like Fran.

"*Oh.*" Benny looked very pleased.

"I didn't see Santa Claus," Marcy said.

"Silly. You don't see Santa Claus," Kathy said. "He's there and gone before you know it."

"I saw him," Benny said. "I talked to him, too. He came into my *house.*"

"That was special," Jo said. "I'll bet he thought you were asleep, and you surprised him."

"Yeah, I did." Benny tugged on his hat. "I s'prised him."

"Lucky ducky!" Kathy said.

"Well, let's get over to that cabin while the storm's died down a bit," Dave said.

"Has he eaten any dinner yet, Claire?" Fran asked.

"I don't know."

"Well, let's have everybody take something. The poor boy needs food, after all."

Jo began to grin as the party got organized, with each person wrapping up his or her favorite part of the meal to take to Russ. She chose to take nothing. She had something to give him besides dinner.

Once they were in the van, with the aroma of food wafting around them, Lucile spoke up. "Let's go in one group at a time, in the same order as Russ showed up at our houses. I'll be first."

"And we'll be last," Fran said.

"No, I'll be last," Jo said.

"Oh." Fran glanced at her with a secret smile. "Right."

"We have time for one Christmas carol," Claire said. She started "We Wish You a Merry Christmas," which they just had time to finish before they pulled up in front of the small log cabin with a single light burning in the window.

Jo sat by the van window, her hands clenched in her lap as Steve helped Lucile down the steps of the van and over to Russ's door. Lucile was a good choice for the first visitor. Russ wasn't likely to close the door in the older woman's face.

The door opened and Russ looked surprised to see Steve and Lucile there. Jo couldn't hear what they said, but Lucile went inside and Steve hopped back in the van.

"He's completely kerflummoxed," Steve said, grinning.

When Lucile reappeared, Ned and Sharon jumped from the van. Ned helped Lucile back on board while Sharon knocked on Russ's door.

"What a sweet boy," Lucile said. "He asked about the kittens."

"I think it's stopped snowing enough to take Amanda in to see him, don't you, Jo?" Elaine asked.

"Absolutely. He needs to see Amanda," Jo said. Her stomach felt as if she'd swallowed Mexican jumping beans.

Hector Barnes tapped Jo on the shoulder. "This is sort of like that movie, you know?"

Jo gazed at him as if the concept was brand new to her. "Is it really?"

"Yeah. We're all reminding him of how he helped us out, to cheer him up. That's what that angel did for Jimmy Stewart."

Claire squeezed Jo's arm. "Let's hope it works."

"Let's hope." Jo grew more and more nervous as the trail of visitors continued and her turn drew near. Finally, Fran and the girls climbed back into the van while Steve and Ned helped Dave in through the back.

"I told him to snatch you right up," Fran said as she passed Jo.

Jo's stomach churned. "Thanks, I think. Does he seem...upset?"

"He seems totally confused," Fran said. "But I'm sure you can straighten him out."

"Go get him, Clarence," Claire said.

Jo paused before leaving the van. "Listen, Steve, why don't you take everybody on home? I may be a while."

"I hope you are." He winked at her. "Good luck."

"Merry Christmas, Jo!" called Lucile from the back of the van.

A chorus of Merry Christmases followed Jo as she stepped from the van. The swirling snow felt good against her flushed cheeks. She had no idea what she'd say to Russ, but she knew it would be the most important speech of her life.

She knocked on the door.

He opened it, showing no surprise at seeing her there. "I figured you'd be at the end of the train." He didn't sound angry, or even impatient. He stepped back. "Come on in, sweetheart."

"Don't call me that unless you mean it," she blurted out, storming into the room and whirling to face him. She hadn't known what to say before, but she did now. "Don't call me your *honey*, or *little darlin'*, or anything like that unless I'm the last one of those you're ever going to have. And you'd be a fool not to take me, Russ, because I'm the best thing that ever happened to you, and I'm sick of you not being able to see that!" She paused to gulp in a breath.

The one-room cabin was filled with the scents of Christmas dinner piled on the small table in the corner. Russ stood partly in shadow, his arms crossed over his chest. "Go on. I can tell you're not played out yet."

"No, I'm not! You lived through that crash, but so what? You might as well not have. It's terrible the way you've denied your love to folks these past three years. You have so much love to give, and you keep it bottled up inside, never letting Steve know how much you care about him, or Claire, or..."

"Or you?" he said softly.

She swallowed hard. "Or me."

He uncrossed his arms and stepped closer, although his face was still in shadow. "All those folks who came to visit me tonight. Was that your idea?"

She lifted her chin. "Yes, it was. You gave love to those people last night, whether you realized it or not. Some of them were strangers to you. If you can do that, then the least you can do is love the people closest to you."

"Like you?"

She met his gaze, but the light was too dim for her to read the emotion written there. "Yes, like me."

"Did you ask them all to tell me that?"

She stared at him in shock. "T-tell you what?"

"That I'd be a damn fool if I didn't snap you up quick as I could."

"No!" Heat rose to her already flushed cheeks. "Of course I wouldn't ask them to say such a thing. I just thought they'd like to thank you for being Santa Claus last night."

"Well, they did that, and then every last one of them told me to marry you. Even the kids."

"Oh, Russ." She covered her face in embarrassment. "I really didn't—" She paused and took her hands away to gaze at him defiantly. "But it's true. You should."

His mouth twitched as if he might be holding back a smile. "And why should I?"

"You're a smart man, Russ, and you should have figured it out by now. If you haven't, I'm sure not going to tell you!"

He stepped more fully into the light, and there, in the depths of his eyes, was the same glow she'd seen when he'd come into the kitchen this afternoon. "Okay, I'll take a stab at it. Maybe because I don't want to end up alone and miserable like Hector Barnes, or maybe because I'd like to have a little girl like Amanda someday, or a little boy like Benny."

Her heart started beating in a crazy rhythm.

"Maybe because I want to be with you when you pay Lucile and the kittens a visit, and maybe because I want that special something that Ned has with Sharon, and Fran has with Dave. Maybe because nobody's ever done something like this for me, sent a whole army of folks to convince me I'm a good person." He smiled. "And maybe because you're the prettiest thing stark naked that I've ever seen."

His last comment heated her blood. "Russ!"

"And maybe because I love hearin' you say my name." He took her gently into his arms. "And maybe because I want to keep callin' you sweetheart, and little darlin' and honey for the rest of my life. And because Ned said he'd kill me if I didn't marry you, and then he'd go to jail and Sharon would be all alone."

She drank in every word, but still it wasn't enough. "That's all?"

He laughed softly. "That's a powerful lot of reasons, sweetheart." He pulled her closer so that she could feel the wild beating of his heart. "And I didn't have sense enough to see a one of them before. But even taking all those reasons, there's still something missing, isn't there?"

"Yes." Her world hung in the balance as she waited.

"Then I guess I should marry you because I love you more than life itself. Be my wife, Jo. Help me start livin' again."

She started to cry.

"Oh, little darlin', don't cry." He kissed her cheeks, her eyes, her mouth. "Please don't."

"I'm...crying...because I'm...really, really *happy*," she said through her tears.

"Happy tears? Like Lucile's?"

"Y-yes." She sniffed.

"Then I must have given you something special."

She gazed up at him through watery eyes. "Only the best Christmas present of my life."

"Does that mean you like the idea of gettin' married and making love to each other for the rest of our born days?"

"I love it. It's the right kind, the right color and it fits great. That's why I'm crying."

He swept her up in his arms and carried her to the bed. "Then get ready to sob your little eyes out, honey. Because all I'm gonna do for the next sixty or seventy years is give you that same present over and over and over again."

KEY TO MY HEART

Unlock the secrets of romance just in time for the most romantic day of the year— Valentine's Day!

Key to My Heart features three of your favorite authors,

**Kasey Michaels,
Rebecca York
and Muriel Jensen,**

to bring you wonderful tales of romance and Valentine's Day dreams come true.

As an added bonus you can receive Harlequin's special Valentine's Day necklace. FREE with the purchase of every *Key to My Heart* collection.

Available in January,
wherever Harlequin books are sold.

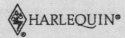

It's hot...
and it's out of control!

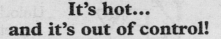

BLAZE

This January, Temptation turns up the
heat. Look for these bold, provocative,
ultra-sexy books!

NIGHT HEAT
by Lyn Ellis

Tripp Anderson had been hired to protect
beautiful, sexy, *rich* Abby Duncan. Keeping his
gorgeous client safe wasn't hard—keeping his
hands off her *was*. But when Abby was threatened,
Tripp vowed to look after her, even if it meant
keeping watch day and night. Little did he expect
his night *watch* to become night *heat*....

BLAZE! Red-hot reads from Temptation!

HARLEQUIN®

Temptation

THE MEN OF BACHELOR CREEK

Alaska. A place where men could be men—and women were scarce!

To Tanner, Joe and Hawk, Alaska was the final frontier. They'd gone to the ends of the earth to flee the one thing they all feared—MATRIMONY. Little did they know that three intrepid heroines would brave the wilds to "save" them from their lonely bachelor existences.

Enjoy

#662 CAUGHT UNDER THE MISTLETOE!
December 1997

#670 DODGING CUPID'S ARROW!
February 1998

#678 STRUCK BY SPRING FEVER!
April 1998

by Kate Hoffmann

Available wherever Harlequin books are sold.

HARLEQUIN® *Temptation*

A showgirl, a minister—
and an unsolved murder.

EASY VIRTUE

Eight years ago Mary Margaret's father was
convicted of a violent murder she knew he
didn't commit—and she vowed to clear his
name. With her father serving a life sentence,
Mary Margaret is working as a showgirl in Reno
when Reverend Dane Barrett shows up with
information about her father's case. Working to
expose the real killer, the unlikely pair also
proceed to expose themselves to an unknown
enemy who is intent on keeping the past buried.

**From the bestselling author of
LAST NIGHT IN RIO**

JANICE KAISER

Available in December 1997
at your favorite retail outlet.

MIRA
BOOKS

The Brightest Stars in Women's Fiction.™

DEBBIE MACOMBER

invites you to the

HEART OF TEXAS

Join Debbie Macomber as she brings you the lives
and loves of the folks in the ranching community
of Promise, Texas.

If you loved Midnight Sons—don't miss
Heart of Texas! A brand-new six-book series
from Debbie Macomber.

Available in February 1998
at your favorite retail store.

Heart of Texas by Debbie Macomber

Lonesome Cowboy	February '98
Texas Two-Step	March '98
Caroline's Child	April '98
Dr. Texas	May '98
Nell's Cowboy	June '98
Lone Star Baby	July '98

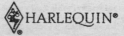

HARLEQUIN®

HPHRT1